# love
# &
# leftovers

# love
# &
# leftovers

*a novel in verse*

## sarah tregay

KATHERINE TEGEN BOOKS
*An Imprint of* HarperCollins *Publishers*

Katherine Tegen Books
is an imprint of HarperCollins Publishers.

Library of Congress Cataloging-in-Publication Data

Tregay, Sarah.
  Love and leftovers : a novel in verse / by Sarah Tregay. — 1st ed.
    p. cm.
  Summary: When her father starts dating a man, fifteen-year-old Marcie's
depressed mother takes her to New Hampshire but just as Marcie starts
falling for a great guy her father brings her back to Idaho, where all of her
relationships have become strained.
  ISBN 978-0-06-202358-2 (trade bdg.)
  [1. Novels in verse. 2. Interpersonal relations—Fiction. 3. Family problems—
Fiction. 4. Moving, Household—Fiction. 5. Bisexuality—Fiction. 6. New
Hampshire—Fiction. 7. Idaho—Fiction.] I. Title.
PZ7.5.T74Love 2012
[Fic]—dc23
                                                    2011019367
                                                         CIP
                                                          AC

Typography by Joel Tippie
12 13 14 15 16  LP/RRDH  10 9 8 7 6 5 4 3 2 1
❖
First Edition

*For high school Leftovers everywhere*

# love
# &
# leftovers

*part one*

DURHAM, NEW HAMPSHIRE

# My Family's Summerhouse

My mother
doesn't understand
that this is a summerhouse
(meant to be lived in
only during the summer).

It is almost Labor Day.

Next week,
I'll start my sophomore year
at Oyster River High School
in Durham, New Hampshire,

because she doesn't have the courage
to go home
to Boise, Idaho.

## The Breakup

On the first Saturday in June,
Mom and I stopped at Albertsons
to buy milk and bananas.

We bumped into Dad,
who was on his way out—
a Coke in his hand.

But Mom forgot about the
milk and bananas when
Dad introduced us
to a friend of his named Danny,
a bartender at the straight-friendly
establishment across from the opera.

Mom's eyes narrowed
and her face hardened into granite.
Then she shot the two of them
a look hot enough

to melt flesh.

# Long Shot

Mom grabbed my wrist,
pulled me across the parking lot,
and told me to get in the car.

She sank into the driver's seat
and I watched the granite crumble
into ragged breaths and searing tears.

"What is it?" I whispered.

"I can't believe it," my mother said,
more to the windshield than to me.
"Seventeen goddamned years!"

(That was how long Dad and Mom had been married.)

She never did answer my question.
She did, however, start in on a blue streak
that lasted until she pulled into the driveway.

So I pieced together the information.
Dad'd been going out for drinks a lot lately.

Danny worked at a straight-friendly bar,
which was probably a nice way to say *gay bar*.
Dad said he and Danny were friends.
And that pissed Mom off.

Now Mom was swearing about
how long she had been married to Dad,
as if today was the last day
she'd consider herself his wife.

"Is Dad gay?" I wondered out loud, hoping
my problem-solving skills weren't very good
and that I'd missed the mark by a thousand miles.

But Mom nodded yes.

## An Explanation

My mother
took two weeks off
back in June.

I asked her
(in July)
what we were doing.

I think she meant to say, "Vacationing"
but she said, "Running away."

Which might have been okay,
even though I thought that
if I ever ran away,
I'd do it with
a certain emo-sensitive rocker boy
and not my mother.

## *Lonely*

The worst part of
this overextended summer vacation
is leaving

behind

a perfectly good boyfriend
with the deepest
espresso-brown eyes
a girl
could ever
get lost
in.

## Since the Breakup

      my mother
      has transported herself
to another world.

On her planet
      showers,
      waking up before sunset,
      matching her clothes,
      and leaving the house
are optional.

Meanwhile
      typing furiously,
      crying constantly,
      and pitting coffee against sleeping pills
      for a battle over her body
are commonplace.

Sometimes
      I think she needs
      those antidepressants
      we see in TV commercials.

But every time an ad comes on
she changes the channel.

So she needs me
    making her toast,
    washing her clothes,
    buying her groceries,
and bringing her Kleenex.

## Saturday at the Laundromat

My mother sleeps late
almost every day
because being asleep
is better than
being depressed.

On Saturday she forgets
that the fridge is empty,
our clothes are dirty,
and the towels smell
from too many dips in the bay.

So I pilfer change
from the cup holder of Dad's car
(which Mom drove here to make him mad)
and walk three miles into town
with a pillowcase of laundry
over one shoulder.

Filling a washer
with my clothes, the towels,
and a few of Mom's underthings,

I line up eight quarters
and slide them in all at once.

I sit outside the Laundromat
and watch the college students
walk by in UNH T-shirts,
miniskirts made from jeans,
and form-fitting sweats
with *wildcats* printed on the ass.

They seem dislocated—
as if they hope
that a large cappuccino,
ten pounds of art history books,
*Jane Eyre*, and Toni Morrison's *Song of Solomon*
will help them find their way.

And looking at them,
I understand how they feel.

Lost.

## *Every Time Dad Calls and Mom Answers*

she tells him that she doesn't want to talk
but she doesn't hang up.

She asks him:     How?     Why?     When?

As I listen in on the other phone,
he tries to explain
that he felt alone
in their marriage—
that they hadn't been
close in a long time.

Mom informs him
that he is a husband
and a father
and that maybe he should
think about the people in his life
a little more.

He says
he wants to
see his daughter

and maybe she could think
about driving his Mustang back to Boise
sometime soon.

My mother goes ballistic
shouting swearing crying
until the mechanical voice
informs us,
"If you'd like to make a call,
please hang up and dial again."

## I Want to Ask Dad Questions Too

Why     is he gay now and not before?
Why     is this bartender guy so special?
Why     did he start down one road,
           only to take the left fork
           at the last minute?
Why     did he break up our family?

But when we're talking on the phone,
my brain churns and my mouth opens,
but no questions come out,
as if my words are swept away by the tide.

"Are you there, Marcie?" Dad asks.

I let a few waves tug at the dock,
before I say, "I'm here."

Even though I'm not.

I'm not home. I'm not with him.
I'm not even sure I understand.

"I love you, Sugar Cookie," Dad says.

My eyes sting with almost tears,
and I want to ask him to say it again,
because I'm not so sure anymore.

"I love you too," I say
before we say good-bye.

# The First Day of School

My mother is awake,
making me pancakes
on the one burner
that still works.

I sit by the fire
in the potbellied stove,
fluffing my short brown hair
so it will dry faster.

"I can drive you to school," she says.
But because she has adopted
that I-don't-care-what-men-think approach
and is wearing two T-shirts
but no bra,
I say, "No thanks."

I walk down our lane
and wait for the school bus
in solitude.

But the bus driver
doesn't stop for me.

I contemplate running after it.
Then decide
that would be more embarrassing
than my mother.

## The Second Day of School

I apologize to the principal
for my mother's
airheaded moments,
like not registering me for school.

I tell him we drove to
the free clinic in Manchester
after the school secretary explained
that I needed a physical.

And that my mother
had forgotten
my immunization records
(back in Idaho)
and they had to be faxed.

And that is why
my first day of school
is everyone else's
second.

## Talk about Accents

People from Idaho
don't really have accents.
We could all be news anchors
because we sound so vanilla.

People from New England
are another story.

My mother grew up here
with her sister, Greta.
She used to leave the *r*'s
off the ends of words that needed them (like *New Hampshire*)
and add them to words that don't (like *idea*).

Yep, Mom used to say "I got an idear!
Let's go to New Hampshah."
Now, she just gets in the car and starts driving.

Mom got tired of people
not understanding what she said.
So she learned to talk
like a news anchor from Idaho.

## *The Teachers Hate*

that I have messed up
their seating charts,
their textbook counts,
and the neat, alphabetized
list of names
in their grade books.

They ask me my name.     "Marcie Foster."

"Mahcie Fostah?"          I nod.

"That's not what it says heah."   "I know."

"It says Mahtha Iris Fostah."   Named after two
                                 grandmothers.

Each time I hope
that they will mangle
my old-fashioned name
so badly that no one
will know
what it really is.

## "*Martha Iris?*"

a voice asks
in the hall
while I am trying
to find my history class.

I turn to say hi to
the first person my age
to acknowledge my existence.

A goth girl
with maroon lipstick
and once-black hair
that has faded to shades
of purple, gray, and blue
looms over me.

"Uh, hi—"

    "Sam."

"Hi, Sam. I'm Marcie."

"I like Martha Iris better,
   it sounds so eighteenth century."

"Uh, thanks?"

# *I Know I Shouldn't Put People in Boxes*

or classify them into cafeteria table categories,
but I can't help myself.

I can tell
Sam isn't the type to sit with the jockettes.
Maybe with the drama freaks or the stoners.

Or maybe she is like me
and my friends back home
who don't fit in anywhere.
Leftovers.

Maybe Leftovers can spy Leftovers
one hundred yards away.
And that is why she said hello to me.

But the problem is
I don't want to be just any old Leftover.
If I can't sit with my friends,
I don't want to be a Leftover.
I want to fit in.

So, even though I spy
Sam's multicolored locks
on the other side of the cafeteria,
I find a different table and ask, "Is this seat taken?"
hoping for the best.

Everyone is friendly,
but I can't follow a single conversation.
It's like they are continuing
their discussion from yesterday.
The girls talk about modeling class
and dressage horses imported from Ireland.
The boys reenact a soccer game
play by play, in excruciating detail
like sportscasters caught in an infinite loop.

# *Things I Left Behind in Boise, Poem 1:*

## MY BEST FRIEND

Katie is adopted.

And her parents are really cool about it.
They always told her that it's okay
to be different—
from your parents,
from your peers—
and Katie took this to heart.

She has a collection of wild-colored socks.
She'll wear one striped one,
and one argyle,
and look at you cross-eyed
if you say something.

She plays the bass guitar—
sometimes so loud the floor joists hum—
but mostly because it's not a chick instrument,
and therefore totally different.

She's taking Japanese for her foreign language
instead of Spanish like the rest of us
because she loves reading manga,
drawing pictures of the characters,
and writing and illustrating her own graphic novels.

Katie has blond hair, wide blue-gray eyes,
and the kind of figure guys notice,
which is all too ordinary for her tastes.
So she dyes colored streaks in her hair,
sometimes blue, sometimes pink.

And her very cool parents
even let her get a tattoo.
So one of Katie's butt cheeks
has the Japanese word for love
gracing its curve.

# Things I Left Behind in Boise, Poem 2:

## MY BOYFRIEND

Linus is not adopted.
But sometimes he wishes he was
(by a different family).

He has three older brothers
    two are in college (majoring in drinking and girls)
    and the oldest, Roland, is a manager at McDonald's
    (who leaves his daughter at his parents' house
        for Linus to babysit).

Linus walks in his brothers' shadows,
    but he isn't loud and obnoxious,
    nor a jock on the football team,
    nor scraping by with Cs.

Unlike his brothers,
    Linus is quiet, and genuinely sweet,
    prefers music to team sports,
    has a 4.0, and doesn't have to shave.

This makes him the perfect boyfriend because he
    holds my hand in the halls
        and whispers little secrets in my ear,
    writes me songs and sings them softly
        while we rock Roland's baby to sleep,
    helps me with my math homework
        and rewards right answers
        with smooth-cheeked kisses.

Oh, and youngest siblings are the best because they
    are never on their parents' radar
        and can do whatever they want,
    are missing that switch
        that turns them into bossy, older-brother jerks,
    wear hand-me-down clothes
        that are all soft and huggable.

# Things I Left Behind in Boise, Poem 3:

## MY FATHER

My father has always been
a little too good-looking
    cleft chin | floppy bangs | clean-shaven
    blue eyes | white smile | a touch of a tan

a little too well-dressed
    cotton shirt | gabardine slacks | silk tie
    wool sweater | cashmere scarf | leather jacket

a little too neat
    knives | forks | spoons
    paper | plastic | aluminum

a little too gay?
    good-looking | well-dressed | perfect.

# Things I Left Behind in Boise, Poem 4:

## THE LEFTOVERS

My friends and I don't fit
into any high-school sitcom caste system.
And we really don't care.
We have each other,
even if the others think we're:

too smart to be jocks,
    Angelo is a geeky numbers guy
    who is also on the swim team.
    He's both sincere and funny,
    and a blast to be around.

too pretty to be losers,
    Emily is a beauty.
    She had a baby freshman year
    and gave him up for adoption.
    I used to want to be Emily.
    Now I'm glad I'm not.

too nice to be popular,
Olive is a Girl Scout.
She goes camping with Brownies for the fun of it.
She's happy and bubbly, and will be the best
camp counselor ever.

too self-conscious to be cheerleaders,
Carolina is compulsive about what she eats.
She counts every calorie and wears padded bras
to compensate for her lack of curves.
I get where she's coming from—
a chubby childhood—and she gets me.

too athletic to be nerds,
Garrett is Olympics material.
He rides his bicycle fifty miles a day
and talks a mile a minute.
He's cute in that jock-meets-geek kind of way.

and too clean to be stoners.
Ian is thoughtful, generous, and a vegetarian,
but hates that we know these things about him.
He'd rather be known for his mad drum skills.

# Things I Left Behind in Boise, Poem 5:

## MY SECURITY BLANKET

Everyone says
I am too old
for a security blanket.

But a baby blanket
tucked in my
dresser drawer back home
is a lot
less expensive
than
psychotherapy.

And I'm
starting to think
that I should have
brought it
with me.

# Things I Left Behind in Boise, Poem 6:

## MY BABY FAT

I was a pale, chubby child
with permanent teeth that seemed too big for my face—
a combination ripe for jokes and embarrassment.
It was like I was destined to be a Leftover.

I wore too-big sweatshirts to hide my pudge
and closed my lips tight over my teeth.
Which didn't win me friends.

Only Katie could make me smile.
And although she, Olive, and Carolina were friends first,
I became her BFF.
We didn't know it in sixth grade,
but we were slowly becoming Leftovers.

Sure, I grew taller
and my round tummy became breasts, hips and thighs.
Sure, I got my braces off
and my teeth no longer seemed too big for my face.

So by the time I finished junior high
I looked normal.
Not pretty or skinny, just average.
But I had already been labeled a Leftover.

## When My Mother Takes an Ambien

I have eight hours to devote to whatever I choose.

Some nights, I take her laptop
down to the end of the lane
to pick up a Wi-Fi signal from the neighbors,
IM Katie, and watch Linus's music videos.

Other nights, I sit facing the glowing coals
and read steamy romance novels that Aunt Greta
has left behind.

Without Mom to tell me
to get off the computer,
or to come inside unless I want West Nile,
I can hang out with my friends (online).

Without Mom to tell me
that weak female characters
are the result of an unimaginative author,
I can read about women who go weak in the knees
at the sight of a cowboy in Levis
and nothing else.

But most of the time
I write poems in this blue notebook
because
I feel free
when Mom is out cold.

## The Worst Thing
## I Have Ever Done

was lie to my parents
and say
it was a girls-only
slumber party
in Katie's backyard.

No.

We didn't do anything
that we needed condoms for
because
Olive, Katie, and Carolina
Garrett, Angelo, and Ian
were there.

## The Best Thing
## Linus Ever Did

was sneak out of the house
and crash
the sleepover/campout,
spending the night
in my sleeping bag.

And,

to tell you the truth,
we couldn't really
move
with two people
in one
Snoopy sleeping bag.

## Driver's License Daydreams

When Linus calls

      I take the cordless outside on the porch.

"I wish you were here," he says.
"I've never had my own room before,
 and it's kind of lonely."

      "Maybe I'll move in," I say.

"You wouldn't want to.
 My dad's gonna lose his job.
 Roland's working double shifts.
 And I'm on constant babysitting duty."

      "I dunno. Might be okay."

"Mom and Dad were joking
 about charging Roland rent.
 And I said he should pay me, too.
 Roland said he'd trade
 babysitting for driving lessons."

"Free drivers' ed? That's great!"

"And he'll let me borrow his car."

"Road trip?"

"Maybe we can go to Bruneau."

"And go sledding on the sand dunes."

We toss ideas back and forth
until Roland's Honda has seen Canada,
Mexico, and every state in between.
And, like all of our conversations,
it reminds us that we are miles apart
when we'd rather be close together.

"This long-distance thing sucks," he says

as if he read my mind.

## The Boat

My mother gives me money
to pick up some dinner
in order to celebrate
the first draft of her novel.

"No," I say. "I have homework.
And I'm tired of running your errands
when you're the one with a driver's license!"

She looks at me funny, then says,
"Just take the boat"                    "Huh?"

"into Newmarket"                        "What?"

"for lobsters."                         "Lobsters?"

I didn't know you could go
anyplace useful in a boat.
I'm from Idaho,
where boats are for
fishing, waterskiing, and boogie boarding.
Not errands.

"I thought that was how
you were doing groceries," Mom says.

I don't tell her
I've been walking into Durham
when all I had to do
was borrow the boat.

# I Don't Like Lobster Anyway

I sulk
on the dock
bobbing on the waves
until
my mother
promises
me
pizza.

## Dominoes

Do you hate the person
    who tapped the first domino down?

Or do you hate the domino
    for not standing up for itself?

And if you are the second domino,
    and you get toppled, do you hate yourself?

    Dad tapped the first domino
    by opening the proverbial closet.

    Mom fell over.

    And me? I toppled too.
    (And landed on the far side of the continent.)

But I can't hate my dad
just because he's gay.
I love him.

Nor can I leave Mom
when she's so down.
She needs me.

And this
pile of dominoes
is *not* my fault.

## Half-and-Half

Half the time I'm angry with Dad
for opening up that closet door
and letting the whole mess spill out.

If I could, I'd push it back:
    his change of heart,
    his boyfriend Danny,
    the mess he made of our family.

    I'd slam the door and lock it tight.

Half the time I'm mad at Mom
for running from Pandora's box
and not finding her way back home.

If I could, I'd break her free:
    from her depression,
    her ideas about independence,
    her East Coast childhood haunts.

    I'd bash the bolts and bust her chains.

## Oyster River High School

isn't so bad
(once the bus driver picks you up).
At least no one has pointed out
that wearing the same outfit more than once
and/or
wearing white shorts after Labor Day
is some sort of fashion faux pas.

In fact,
J.D.,
a bulky soccer player with
boy-next-door dimples,
sandy red hair, and a Prince Harry grin,
who sits at my lunch table,
thinks I'm into sports.

I should say, "Not really,"
but instead, I tell him, "Distance,"
and hope he thinks cross-country
instead of walking into Durham
for groceries and laundry.

# The Leftover Lovers YouTube Performance #1

(LINUS THOMAS ON GUITAR/VOCALS,
KATIE RASKOLNIKOV ON BASS,
AND IAN WONG ON DRUMS)

*I see couples riding double on a Schwinn bike*
*I think of you and I know what I like*
*I'm sitting in the back of class*
*Picking my nose and thinkin' past*

*Boise High School auditorium*
*Dancing barefoot in the gym*
*Westside Drive-In, the Egyptian*
*Gene Harris Band Shell*
*Blue Sky Bagels*

*I see brunette girls laughin' in the library*
*I think of you and think of me*
*Eating pancakes at the IHOP*
*I think of you and have to stop*

*Boise High School auditorium*
*Dancing barefoot in the gym*

*Westside Drive-In, the Egyptian*
*Gene Harris Band Shell*
*Blue Sky Bagels*

*I think of you and know what I like*
*I think of you ridin' double on my Schwinn bike*
*I think of you and know what I like*

## I Know I Like Him

I know
Linus is my boyfriend
and he's adorable
in his own Linusy ways.

I know
he's my second-best friend
who'd tie for first
if it wouldn't hurt Katie's feelings.

I know
how smart he is
and that he'd trade it all in
for an ounce of athletic ability.

I know
his music is like my poetry—
an inward glance and
an outlet for expression.

I know
we could be made-for-TV soul mates

who fall ass-over-teakettle
in crazy, amazing love.

I know
I like resting my head on his shoulder
while we watch movies
on the couch.

I know
I like kissing him in the hall between classes
while everyone else
tries not to see.

But how do I know
when it's love?

# A Feeling Like Falling

Katie says, "You can't choose the time and place
 the when and where
 and with whom
 you fall in love."

She says, "It just happens
 like that weird feeling just before you fall asleep
 when you gasp in surprise because your
 muscles just relaxed
 and you feel like you are falling."

She says, "Marcie, you shouldn't
 worry about it—
 give it time
 to actually happen."

I guess,
I worry that I won't do it right.
 That it'll be the wrong time,
 the wrong place,
 the wrong person.

I mean,
I *am* related to my father
who fell in love
    when he was already married
    at the straight-friendly bar across from the opera
    with a *guy* named Danny.

## If Only We Could Be Together

If only Linus and I could walk downtown on
Thursday nights
    when musicians play on the street corners
    and art galleries serve crackers and cheese.
If only we could dance on the sidewalk,
    look up at the sequined sky,
    and wish upon the same shooting star.

If only Linus could teach me chords on his guitar,
    reach around to adjust my fingers
    and help me strum.
If only we could sing about autumn mist and sealing wax,
    hear our voices mingle,
    and stir the air as one.

And by being with Linus
    I'd figure it out.
    I'd learn what love is.
If only Linus would kiss me,
    touch the skin under my shirt,
    press his fingers to my ribs, and feel my beating heart.

Then I'd know.
    I know I'd know.
I'd know
    I was in love.

## America Runs on Dunkin'

On a Monday
in mid-September,
J.D. brings me a Boston cream doughnut
and coffee in a pink-and-orange Styrofoam cup.
He tells me not to worry,
"Carbs burn off at practice."

"Yeah," I agree with a shrug.
"Thanks for breakfast."

J.D. smiles down at me
and doesn't notice Sam
passing us in the crowded hall.

She rolls her eyes skyward
and shakes her head.

Later, I'm shaking mine too
because I can't quite believe
that J.D. thinks
I am skinny enough
to be a runner.

Then I remember
that ever since we ran away,
the fridge hasn't always
been full of carbs.

## Give Me a Break, Sam

I am not some horrible person.
I was just talking to him—
not batting my eyelashes
or pulling some *CosmoGirl*
how-to-hook-a-hottie move.

A lot of girls (and some guys)
would think J.D. was cute.

Any girl with a pulse
would've wanted to brush that
powdered sugar from his lips.

Sure, I have a boyfriend.
A wonderful, sweet, talented boyfriend.

But Linus isn't here right now.

So give me a break.

# Talking to Linus Is Depressing

Linus tells me about his music lessons,
then puts me on speaker and strums his guitar.
I can hear him singing softly to keep the beat.

> *Hmm, hmm come September*
> *Hmm, hmm I'll remember*
> *All those sunny days I spent with you*
>
> *Hmm, hmm come October*
> *Hmm, hmm I'll be sober*
> *Every lonely evening without you*
>
> *Hmm, hmm come November*
> *Hmm, hmm I'll reconsider*
> *Walking down the highway to reach you*
>
> *Hmm, hmm come December*
> *Hmm, hmm I'll be dismembered*
> *by the snowplow passing through*

"Linus!" I shout into the phone. "Stop it!"

"Those aren't the real words," he promises me.
"I forgot the words and made something up.
What did you think of the guitar, sans words?"

All I can say is that it sounds nice,
and I really miss watching his fingers move over the strings
because that was my favorite part
of having an emo-rocker boyfriend.

"Favorite?" he asks.

"I also liked the kissing," I say.
It doesn't come out funny, or flirty, or however I meant it.

It just reminds us that we're having
a long-distance relationship.

The kind everyone says
is doomed from the start.

# BFF

Sometimes I want
nothing more
than to be writing poems
in my blue notebook

while Katie doodles
anime ninja girls
battling bat-winged
skeletons with vampire fangs
in hers.

I want to
trade notebooks with Katie
so my poems will grow emo vines
with bloodthirsty flowers

and her ninja girls will voice
their anger and
odd romantic attractions
to the homely monsters.

## HOME Is a Four-Letter Word

Missing Katie,
I tell my mother
that I want to go home.

But all she does is ask me
what kind of mother she would be
if she left her daughter
to fend for herself
2,700 miles away?

I wonder if
I shake her hard enough,
will all the pieces
of her scattered thoughts
fall into place?

## September 14—11:45 p.m.

EmoK8:     if u weren't going out w linus, whose
           bones would u jump?

MarsBars:  *hello 2 u 2*

EmoK8:     i think i need a boyfriend.

MarsBars:  *All this talk about falling in love, now u
           want some?*

EmoK8:     u got me thinking.

MarsBars:  *as long as ur not worrying abt it. \*grin\**

EmoK8:     i'm not worrying. i need advice.

MarsBars:  *good-looking guys are, well, nice to look at.
           but homely ones can be sexy too—
           so don't rule em out.*

EmoK8:     i need some lovin.
           who's a good kisser?

MarsBars:  *i kissed angelo in 8th grade.
           it was slobbery.*

EmoK8:     who's better looking, angelo or garrett?

MarsBars:  *naked?*

EmoK8:     u've seen them naked?

MarsBars:  *no. overactive imagination. angelo.*

EmoK8:     but garrett shaves his legs when he races.
           u don't think that's hot?

| | |
|---|---|
| *MarsBars:* | *angelo shaved everything when he made it to the state swim meet.* |
| EmoK8: | everything? |
| *MarsBars:* | *well, everything that wasn't under his Speedo. remember his bald head?* |
| EmoK8: | that was soooo funny! |
| *MarsBars:* | *i wish linus had to shave. i think i'd like scruffy kisses.* |
| EmoK8: | nah. japanese guys are really hot and they don't shave much. |
| *MarsBars:* | *if you think asian guys are cute, ask ian out.* |
| EmoK8: | ian? |
| *MarsBars:* | *yeah, you two hang out all the time. you'd make sweet rock n roll.* |
| EmoK8: | you'd go out w Ian? |
| *MarsBars:* | *yeah. ian minus the drumming can b really sweet.* |
| EmoK8: | ian's a geek. |
| *MarsBars:* | *so are you. *wink** |
| EmoK8: | i see being in solitary confinement in the NH wilderness has not done anything for ur sense of humor. |
| *MarsBars:* | *very funny. speaking of solitary confinement,* |

> *i should get back to my jailer*
> *b4 she realizes i stole her Mac.*

EmoK8: luv ya bye

*MarsBars:* *luv u 2, nite*

## Speaking of Good-Looking Guys

On the fourteenth Boston cream,
I tell J.D.
that I prefer
glazed sour cream,
or jelly with powdered sugar.

And he says
he might bring me one
if I'd be his date
for the homecoming dance.

And before I say anything,
he goes on to explain
that all school athletes
are strongly encouraged to attend.
"Tradition," he rambles, "is big here
and since you have to go too,
we might as well go together."

"Yeah," I agree,
as if I wasn't totally thrilled
to be asked to the dance.

## Thank God for Football

I had to come clean
so I sat across from J.D.
over slices at Wildcat's,
the UNH game blaring.

"I'm not on the track team,"
I said,
figuring he'd hate me
and save me from saying
the next thing
on my list.

He mumbled through mozzarella
that it was okay.

Which wasn't exactly
what I wanted to hear.

A conversation-halting touchdown
rumbled through the pizza parlor
before
I told J.D. that we'd be going

to the homecoming dance
as just friends.

Which,
now that I think about it,
would have been
a really stupid thing to say.

Because we are
just friends.

## I Don't Have a Dress to Wear

so I ask Mom to take me to the mall in Manchester.
"Even better," she says, and plans a day trip into Boston.

I imagine Filene's Basement
overflowing with satin gowns
and strapless velvet dresses.

I am so happy
    to get Mom
      out of the house
        and weaving
        swerving
      down Boston's
curvy streets,
    that I hardly
      notice we're in
          Aunt Greta's
        neighborhood
instead of the city.

Greta greets us with a smile
as wide as mine.

## The Perfect Dress

The three of us giggle like girlfriends
as Aunt Greta empties her attic
of every dress the Otis/O'Grady girls have ever worn:
>   Great-Grandmother Gigi's black one
>   she wears to funerals
>   Grammie Iris's baby-blue prom dress, circa 1963
>   Aunt Greta's collection of bridesmaid atrocities
>   Mom's ivory wedding dress.

Cautious,
because I don't want to ruin the mood,
I skip past the funeral blacks and the bridal whites
to the blue satin one,
saying that everyone always said,
I look most like Grammie Iris, except for Dad's dark hair.

I slip it on
zip it up
and fluff it out.

In the mirror, I look a bit like Cinderella
crossed with Snow White.

My mother says
it brings out my eyes.

Greta shows me
how a tulle petticoat
fills out the skirt.

Mom and Greta giggle
and squeeze into sassy dresses
just to be silly.

Still wearing our sneakers,
we hop the T at Harvard Square
and ride downtown
to treat ourselves to dim sum.

Careful not to drip
sweet and sour sauce
on our
evening gowns.

## J.D. Picks Me Up

wearing a tuxedo and driving a Jeep.

Mom gives me a look
mixed with admiration
(because she agrees that J.D. looks like a prince)
and concern
(because she thinks that J.D. looks like a player).

I tell her not to worry
and kiss her on the cheek.
(I won't be getting kissed anywhere else myself.)

"Hey," he says as he turns onto the main road.
"Thanks for coming with me tonight."

"No problem," I reply. "It'll be fun."

"You haven't been to an Oyster River dance.
They're a drag if you don't have someone to talk to."

"I was wondering why you asked me."

"Really?" J.D. glances over at me and smiles.
"I thought that much was obvious."

"What's obvious?" I ask.

"I want us to be friends," he says.
"That's why I bring you breakfast."

*Duh!* I say to myself.
God, I'm so stupid—
just because J.D.'s totally hot
doesn't mean he wants to date
every girl who stumbles
into his life.

## Homecoming at OR

is more like a pep rally
with a little lame music
and dancing thrown in.

J.D. doesn't dance so great.
He just kind of stands there
and holds me.

Which makes me think of Linus
and how he dances through life—
his fingers across his guitar strings,
his stocking feet on the Twister mat,
his bare toes on the school gym floor.
The guy even dances onstage.

I don't mind not dancing.
I've been craving human contact,
touch, connection
ever since Mom and I drove away.

"You okay with us being friends?" J.D. asks,
pulling away and looking down at me.

"Yeah," I say, closing the gap again
and resting my head on his shoulder.

I linger in his arms
after the last note has been played
soaking up all the warmth
and hoping it will last

until the next time
someone hugs me.

## October 5—11:54 P.M.

EmoK8:      i did it!

*MarsBars:*   *did what?*

EmoK8:      kissed angelo!!!!!

*MarsBars:*   *how was it?*

EmoK8:      like eating chocolate-covered
            strawberries dipped in whipped cream

*MarsBars:*   *no fair. when i kissed him, we drooled on
            each other.*

EmoK8:      some things get better with age.

*MarsBars:*   *so is he your boyfriend now?*

EmoK8:      sorta

*MarsBars:*   *that's awesome!*

EmoK8:      speaking of boyfriends,
            carolina and I were at the mall.
            we ran into your dad and danny.
            ur dad was so cute,
            he was shopping for your b-day
            and wanted my opinion
            swore i wouldn't tell.

*MarsBars:*   *u hung out w my dad at the mall????*

EmoK8:      he and danny r so adorable.
            they got us Cokes. we talked.

| | |
|---|---|
| *MarsBars:* | *i am so jealous.* |
| | *u kiss angelo minus the drool,* |
| | *then spend time w my dad!* |
| EmoK8: | i told him u missed him |
| | (ur dad, not angelo). |
| *MarsBars:* | *thnx. what do u mean adorable?* |
| EmoK8: | speaking of adorable men, |
| | have u talked 2 linus lately? |
| *MarsBars:* | *it's too depressing.* |
| EmoK8: | i know. his dad lost his job. |
| *MarsBars:* | *not just that.* |
| | *all we talk about is not being together.* |
| | *makes me want to cry.* |
| EmoK8: | on ur way to being emo |
| *MarsBars:* | *no.* |
| EmoK8: | you like emo boys why not b emo? |
| *MarsBars:* | *because my butt's too big for skinny jeans.* |
| EmoK8: | so emo. luv it. |
| *MarsBars:* | *miss u katie. nite.* |
| EmoK8: | luv u 2. |

# I Close Mom's Computer

and creep back down the lane,
alone again in the middle of the night.

I feel more alone than ever,
because I didn't/couldn't
tell Katie about
how beautiful Grammie Iris's dress fit
and how nice it felt to dance/not dance with J.D.

I thought I could.
But I couldn't.

Because she's friends with Linus.
And he might get the wrong idea.

I know I should have explained
to Katie
how J.D. and I had agreed
that we were just friends.

But I'm not really sure
I could explain how

it felt so good to be held,
and kissed on the cheek.

Because it *did* feel good.
Too good.

## Middle-of-the-Night Daydreams

I pile on more blankets to keep out the cold.
Still shivering, I drag them into the front room
and build a fire in the potbellied stove.

Watching the flames,
I see Katie's words on the screen of my mind:
> *speaking of boyfriends . . .*
> *we ran into your dad and danny . . .*
> *they got us Cokes. we talked.*

So it *is* true.
Dad really is gay.

(I wish he wasn't.)

Dad and Danny hang out together—
shop for my birthday present together.

(I wish they wouldn't.)

This gay-dad-depressed-mom craziness
is not a nightmare I can wake up from.

(I wish I could.)

In this universe there are no time machines,
or keys that can turn hearts back around.

(I wish there was.)

If there was a restart button
that'd reboot my parents' relationship

I'd press it.

## Dinner

My mother glances up at me
as she twirls spaghetti.
We share a soft-lipped smile.

I look down
and realize
I twirl noodles
just like she does.

And
in my very next thought
I wonder
if my boyfriend is gay.

That would explain
why he never once
took off
my
clothes.

## When I Was Little

my mother used to tell me
how wonderful my father was
    how smart, how funny.

She used to explain
how perfect it was to share
    books, art, and music.

What she meant was
    don't fall for a hard body
    without a soft heart
like Aunt Greta did.

I ask her, "Do you take it back?"

She doesn't understand
    so I explain about soft hearts.

"Your father had a little more than a midlife crisis.
    I liked his sports car fetish better."

"But do you take it back?"

"No. I still believe in kind men."

"But what if all the nice guys are gay?"
I ask.

"What if Linus is gay?"
I panic.

"If he is," Mom says, "you'll have two best friends."

Crap.

So I waited fifteen years
for some guy to call me his girlfriend.
And he probably has a crush on the quarterback.

# When Dad Calls and I Answer

I take the cordless down the steps to the dock
and hide from my mother.

He asks me when I'll be coming home.

I tell him Mom needs me,
that she's coming unraveled.

"What about you? Are you okay?"

"Yeah. I made a friend. We went to homecoming."

"A guy friend or a girl friend?"

"A guy friend, Dad."

He sighs.
"It's the guy friends of yours I worry about."

I laugh.
"You *and* Mom."

"At least we still agree on some things."
He sighs again, louder this time
and more tired.

"Did I tell you that I cut my hair?"
I say to change the subject.

## "You Cut Your Hair?"

So I had to tell him
the whole haircut story:

It started with a bad hair day.
Because three months of
swimming in Great Bay
and attempting to wash my hair
in the trickle of well water
that resembled a shower,

left my once-straight, long hair
tangled and sticking out like a wilted Afro
and feeling like it was well on its way
to dreadlocking itself.

## Hairapy

My great-grandmother, Gigi, told me that
I should wash it with apple cider vinegar
(because I am a brunette),
and condition it with mayonnaise
(not Miracle Whip),

in order to get
clean,
straight,
shampoo-commercial hair.

Needless to say,

I smelled like
potato salad
for three days.

## Until

I marched into town,
    plunked my butt in the salon chair,
    and told the lady
    to cut it off.

I didn't expect
    her to put the scissors
    between my ponytail holder
    and the back of my head.

I didn't expect
    my hair to fall to the floor
    in just one
    soft *tha-wump*.

My head felt instantly lighter,
    the back of my neck cooler,
    and the smell of salad dressing
    had faded just a little bit.

I didn't expect
    a simple haircut

to change my appearance
so much.

I looked cute,
    almost pretty—
    but vanity embarrasses me.
    So I didn't take a picture
    to send to my boyfriend
    back in Boise.

# Family Hairstory

Aunt Greta informed me
that every single Otis/O'Grady girl
had fallen for the vinegar-and-mayonnaise trick
since Gigi was young.
In 1927.

And even though I had smartened up,
Gigi kept trying to get me to do
things she did when she was my age.

"When I was a young lady,
I sent this young man a lock of my hair,
so he'd remember me."

"That's very *Sense and Sensibility* of you, Gigi."

"You should send a lock to your sweetie."

(I kept my old ponytail to remind myself
not to wash my hair with items from the fridge.)

I knew her mind was getting old-lady foggy,
because I have proof
that she and G'pa traded
sexy pictures of themselves in bathing suits
when he was off at war.

# My Relatives Are Like Grapes on a Vine

Aunt Greta,
Great-uncle Arthur,
Grammie Iris,
and Great-grandmother Gigi
run the world's most efficient grapevine.

Aunt Greta
    considers gossip
    an evening on the town
    over a glass of wine the size of Lake Winnipesaukee
    in one of Boston's finest restaurants.

Uncle Arthur
    loves to play hooky from work,
    stopping at the deli on his way through Durham
    and borrowing a beer from the summerhouse fridge.
    He shares his sandwiches with whomever he finds
    lounging on the porch and watching the tide.

Gigi has a sweet tooth
    that she lies about every time
    she presses a quarter into my palm

and tells me to be a dear
and buy her an ice cream downstairs in the parlor.
Together we lick Blue Bunny,
whispering so her roommate won't hear.

Grammie Iris moved to Bennington
    eons ago
    (to escape the Grapes).
    But because she is away from the vineyard
    everyone calls her and keeps her up-to-date.

Mom used to be like Iris
(when we lived in Boise)
overhearing every word about
    Aunt Greta's divorce,
    Uncle Arthur's fake knee,
    Gigi's moving into a nursing home,
    and Grammie Iris's promotion to professor emerita.

Now the Grapes
    are talking about us.

## *Money*

"Don't turn on the furnace,"
my mother warns
when she and Aunt Greta
head out for the evening.
"Or Gigi will get the bill."

Since my great-grandmother
lives in a nursing home
she gets lots of bills
so she doesn't need
another one for propane.

So I pull on my great-grandfather's
World War II bomber jacket,
and go out in the cold
to fetch firewood.

So that Gigi
won't be reminded
that her great-granddaughter
is living in her summerhouse
in October.

## The Conversation

It takes Aunt Greta
to talk
my mother
into renting an apartment.

Greta said
that the pipes freeze
by Veterans Day
and then you have to
haul a bucket of water
up from the bay
to flush
the toilet.

*MarsBars:*    *i've got sorta good news*

EmoK8:    ur coming home?

*MarsBars:*    *no. we're gonna move out of the summerhouse into an apt.*

EmoK8:    marcie, that's not good news.

       it means ur staying in NH.

*MarsBars:*    *can u at least try & b happy 4 me?*

EmoK8:    i'm sorry. i'll try.

*MarsBars:*    *thnx. lets talk abt you, instead.*

EmoK8:    does PMS get worse when ur totally attracted to a hot guy?

*MarsBars:*    *i don't think so.*

EmoK8:    cause i'm all grumpy,

       yet i want to throw myself @ angelo.

*MarsBars:*    *so do it!*

EmoK8:    can't. got my period.

*MarsBars:*    *sucks to be you.*

EmoK8:    sucks to be all of us.

       wait, does linus know?

*MarsBars:*    *nope. told u 1st.*

EmoK8:    he's gonna be bummed.

*MarsBars:*    *yeah, i guess.*

EmoK8:      he will b.

*MarsBars:*  *do u think he's gay?*

EmoK8:      gay????????????

*MarsBars:*  *he never, like, touches me and stuff.*

EmoK8:      kinda hard to touch u

            when u live 3,000,000,000 miles away.

*MarsBars:*  *no, i mean before.*

EmoK8:      he kisses u.

*MarsBars:*  *but maybe that's not enuf.*

EmoK8:      don't worry about it.

*MarsBars:*  *u sure?*

EmoK8:      yeah, he likes you.

*MarsBars:*  *even long-distance?*

EmoK8:      even 3,000,000,000 miles away. g'nite.

*MarsBars:*  *nite*

## Student Housing

So Mom and I
move into the two-bedroom apartment
over the used-books store
next to campus.

We borrow Gigi's furniture
from the summerhouse.

We take the skillet to make pancakes,
the cereal bowls, and the tarnished silverware.

I say a secret good-bye
to the potbellied stove
because I will miss
toasting marshmallows.

## A Bath at Last

After our suitcases have been lugged up the stairs,
after I find soap, shampoo, and a towel,
and after I scrub the bathtub with dish soap,

I fill the tub,
step out of my clothes
and into the water.

Sleepy warmth envelops me
like a cup of chamomile tea.

I relax
floating up with each breath
and sinking when I exhale,
my nipples bobbing
like buoys
on Great Bay.

# I'll Be Brief

After we moved in,
Aunt Greta brought over
two bags of winter clothes.

It felt as if she hated to think
of Mom and me
having only one suitcase each
of clothes to wear.

One bag had things she didn't wear much—
turtlenecks, jeans, and sweaters.

The other bag had new things—
socks, tights, and old-lady underwear.

"Aunt Greta," I told her,
"No one under the age of thirty
wears briefs,
unless, of course,
they're a guy."

I hate to admit it
but
I like my big panties

because
they don't give me
automatic
wedgies.

# Closing Camp

On the last weekend in October,
it is a family tradition
to prepare the summerhouse
for the winter ahead.

Gigi commands operations
from her post on the porch.

My great-uncle Arthur
maneuvers the boat onto the trailer
while I sit in the cab
and pretend to drive

which I prefer to mopping and dusting,
and picking creepy-crawlies off the patio furniture
before dragging it inside.

## Bedtime

The summerhouse was tucked in
among the trees
sung the lullaby of the tide
splashing on the rocks below.

The only thing
not in place
was the spare key,

dry in my pocket
instead of damp
under the potted fern.

# The Leftover Lovers
## YouTube Performance #2

(LINUS THOMAS ON GUITAR/VOCALS,
KATIE RASKOLNIKOV ON BASS,
AND IAN WONG ON DRUMS)

*Marcie, don't believe what they sold you*
*Don't listen to what they told you*
*Just let me knock on your door*
*Wrap my arms around you*
*Even the score*

*Marcie, don't be a pawn*
*In the games parents play*
*In the hours before dawn*

*Marcie, don't believe what they sold you*
*Don't listen to what they told you*
*Just let me knock on your door*
*Wrap my arms around you*
*Even the score*

*Marcie, it's your father's fault*
*Don't be a captive*
*To your mother's doubt*

*Marcie, don't believe what they sold you*
*Don't listen to what they told you*
*Just let me knock on your door*
*Wrap my arms around you*
*Even the score*

*Marcie, I wanna open your door*
*Wrap my arms around you*
*Even the score*

## What I Want to Do

There were tears in my eyes
when I called Linus.

I told him I wished
he was here to hold me.
That I wished I could
    wrap myself around him,
    tuck myself under his chin, and
    bury myself in his arms.

Linus said
    he wanted the same things.

I didn't say
that I wanted to do all of this
    curled under the covers,
    skin against skin
    with nothing but a condom
    between us.

And I wondered if
    Linus wanted the same things.

## A Package from Katie

Wrapped in pink Saran wrap
And topped with a yellow Post-it
That read
> *I know* Fruits Basket
> *is so yesterday*
> *but I had to get us these.*
> *Luv, Katie*

Inside was a
plaid            pleated
Catholic         Japanese
Saint Mary's     schoolgirl
uniform          skirt.

## October 27—12:02 A.M.

| | |
|---|---|
| *MarsBars:* | *katie! i luv the skirt.* |
| | *thank you!* |
| EmoK8: | does it fit? |
| *MarsBars:* | *yep.* |
| EmoK8: | good. |
| | i thought it might be too tight. |
| *MarsBars:* | *no. i've lost abt 12 pounds.* |
| EmoK8: | OMG! congrats. |
| *MarsBars:* | *thnx. i didn't lose it on purpose.* |
| EmoK8: | who cares? i bet you look good ☺ |
| | i dunno tho, linus likes us chubby girls. |
| *MarsBars:* | *ur not chubby.* |
| | *& i'm still not sure linus likes girls.* |
| EmoK8: | argh. linus likes u. |
| | why don't u believe me? |
| *MarsBars:* | *i dunno.* |
| | *he says it, but—* |
| EmoK8: | he doesn't touch u . . . |
| | yeah. u said. |
| | but he can't. ur in NH. |
| *MarsBars:* | *does angelo touch you?* |
| EmoK8: | yes. |

| | |
|---|---|
| *MarsBars:* | *i mean under ur clothes?* |
| EmoK8: | yeah. |
| *MarsBars:* | *and u didn't tell me?* |
| EmoK8: | how was i supposed to bring that up? angelo gave me a back rub, just not on my back? |
| *MarsBars:* | *OMG! on your front?* *did it feel good?* |
| EmoK8: | oh yeah. |
| *MarsBars:* | *i am so jealous.* *i want linus to like me like that.* *if he's not gay, i mean.* |
| EmoK8: | he does. he will. & im not gonna say it again HE IS NOT GAY!!! |
| *MarsBars:* | *ok ok* *anyway, i got a "history of new england ports" paper to write.* |
| EmoK8: | i guess i can let you go. nite. |
| *MarsBars:* | *thnx for playing the marcie song. Nite.* |

## No One to Clink Glasses With

Now that we live in town
I take myself out for dinner
when Mom doesn't feel like eating.
    Pizza at Wildcat's,
    pitas at the deli,
    salads at the sit-down place.

You don't know what lonely is
until you've asked
for a table for one.

The waitress comes over
to fill your glass and
ask you how your salad tastes
a few times too many.

And you wish
she'd just sit down
and talk.

## Katie Rants on the Phone

"Okay, okay,
all you do is go on and on
about Linus being gay.

So what if he is?
Goody for him.
Really, Marcie,
why should you care?

You like gay people—
you love your dad,
and Danny's a sweet guy."

"But what if I love Linus?" I ask her.

"You love him?"

"I don't know," I tell her. "I might . . . I want to.

But I'm worried that
    if Linus is gay        like my father,
    I'll become depressed    like my mother."

# Regret

My decision not to sit with Sam
    (that tall girl with tie-dyed hair)
comes back to haunt me
as I eat pizza alone
on Halloween night
with zero girlfriends to
watch scary movies with
in all of New England.

Someone changes the channel
and a list of upcoming programs
fills the screen.

Instead of feeling sorry for myself,
I order another slice.
    (To go.)

"Hey," I say to Mom when I get home.
"I brought you dinner."

"Thanks, honey."

"Would you watch TV with me?
*It's the Great Pumpkin, Charlie Brown*
is coming on at seven."
    (Not scary, I know,
        but horror films aren't Mom's thing.)

"I'd love to," she says,
and closes her computer.

# Frat Boys

fill every seat,
scarfing down pizza
and yelling at the flat screen
when some poor sucker
fumbles the ball.

The only subject
that tugs at their attention spans
is a gaggle of coeds
in tight jeans
and tank tops (in November)
who flirt without mercy
flashing Crest Whitestrips smiles
and cleavage.

One girl takes a seat
on the cutest guy's lap.
She steals a slice,
tips her head back,
and laughs.

And I wonder
what it would take
to become one of those girls.
I could
buy my shirts a size too small,
and bleach my teeth until they glow in the dark.

I could laugh at the frat boys' jokes
as I park my butt
on some cute guy's knee.

I wouldn't be me.

But maybe I'd like
taking a break
from myself.

## Clothes

My mother always warned me
that certain combinations
will attract the wrong
kind of attention

like black bras and white T-shirts,
or mascara and miniskirts,
bathing suits with zippers,
or lipstick with high heels.

She's talking about attracting:
    college boys in tight undershirts
        with ponytails and goatees
    lifeguards in red board shorts
        with blue eyes and suntans
    jocks in black Adidas
        with big hands and firm biceps.

It doesn't take me long
to put two and two together,
mix the wrong combinations

like push-up bras and tank tops,
lip gloss and eyeliner,
perfume and a bomber jacket.

Just like the girl
who didn't get in trouble
for stealing a slice of pizza.

# I Love Pizza

The next Friday,
    not a seat in the house
    is without an ass.

J.D. waves me over to an already full table,
    puts his arm around my waist,
    and pulls me down to sit on his lap.

We drink Cokes, eat slices, and watch the Patriots
    run-dodge their way down the field,
    ready to leap up and cheer at a moment's notice.

During commercials
    J.D.'s fingers tickle my thighs
    as he toys with the hem of my skirt.

# Motherly Advice for the Teenage Soul

Mom always told me
    to stand up for myself
    to not put up with rude boys,
    roaming fingers, and wandering hands.

And I always thought I would
    stand up for myself
    and refuse their advances,
    stray strokes, and wayward gropes.

Yet, I am sitting, sipping my soda
    and enjoying every delicious minute of it.

A thought bubbles up
through my carbonated brain:

    Linus.

I brush J.D.'s fingers away from my legs,
    whispering, "Not now,"
    so he won't think that I don't like him
    (I do)

or how he touched me
(I like that too).

I'd tell him that I have a boyfriend, just
not now.

## Treats

The next day at school,
J.D. dangles a paper bag over my head:
"I got something for you."

I consider reaching for the Dunkin' Donuts,
but his T-shirt rides up,

and the
        trail
          of
        blond
          hairs
        trickling
          down
        his
          six-
        pack
          abs

makes me hungry
for other things.

# *Insight*

If my friends and family
were foods,

J.D. would
be dessert,
you know,
like bananas Foster
dripping
with caramel
and

on fire.

## My Birthday

You'd think that my mother would have remembered
that she gave birth to a baby girl sixteen years ago
and wake up to make her pancakes
before school.

You'd think that my mother would have remembered
watching Molly Ringwald blow out her sixteen candles
all those years ago.

But she is tucked in a fog
under a blue comforter
of Ambien and depression.

I even let the phone ring four times,
thinking it sounds like an alarm clock.

"Sugar Cookie, happy birthday!" Dad says.
"I wanted to be the first one to wish you well."

"Don't worry, Daddy,
you were."

# Birthday Presents

J.D. brings me a jelly doughnut
and coffee with cream.

"You wanted a sour cream?" he asks
when I
start to cry.

# At 3:20 That Afternoon Everyone Remembers

On his way to soccer practice,
J.D. promises to take me out for a celebration,
to be ready at eight.

Uncle Arthur picks me up at school
and we swing by the deli
to buy sandwiches.

At our apartment,
Aunt Greta says she left work at noon
to avoid the traffic.

Mom smiles
and wraps a hug around me
to make me forget this morning.

Arthur, Greta, Mom, and I
drive to the summerhouse and build a fire,
to celebrate with birthday sandwiches on the patio
    furniture.

## More Birthday Presents

Greta gives me a big, flat box wrapped in glossy paper.
Inside is a pale ivory parka with a faux fur collar.
I pull it on, zip it up, and tell her she shouldn't have.
"To make up for the panties."

Arthur gives me a yellow envelope,
a gift card to the mall in Manchester.
I thank him, give him a hug, and kiss his scratchy cheek.
"To get there, you'll have to give me a call."

Mom produces a teddy bear from inside a grocery bag.
It's soft and squishy, with caramel fur and chocolate eyes.
I hold it close, feeling like a child as tears threaten.
"To talk to, when I'm not the best listener."

## Three Gifts Are in Blue-and-White Priority Mail Boxes

A blushing pink camisole from Katie.
"To wear to bed. Every girl deserves to feel sexy."

A black Moleskine journal from Linus.
"To replace that blue notebook. Which is probably full."

A pearl necklace from Dad and Danny.
"No need to explain real pearls to real women."

My lawn chair is stacked with gifts,
and I am swirling on an emotional carnival ride,
holding a teddy bear
and wearing a too-fancy necklace with a parka,
wishing Linus had sent me the camisole,
yet glad he didn't

because Mom doesn't think
lingerie is an appropriate gift
for a guy to give a girl.

## After Greta and Arthur Kiss Me Good Night

J.D. picks me up,
and promises my mother
I'll be back by midnight.

He takes me to an oversized house
on Faculty Row
with warm light spilling from windows.

We are greeted with a big "Surprise!"
from J.D.'s friends from school,
his mom and dad,
and a pair of redheaded little girls
who must be his sisters.

"Mahcie!" they shout over the commotion.
"We made you a cake,
shaped like a heart
with pink frosting
and sixteen candles."

And happy sad tears
almost spill

when they show me
the gooey, lopsided cake
topped with pastel candles
ready to be lit.

## My Wish

is to fall
cranium over Converse
in dizzy daydream-worthy
love.

## *After the Guests Have Gone*

J.D. drives me home,
parks the Jeep on the street,
and walks me to the door
long before midnight.

"Thank you," I tell him.
"You didn't have to do that."

"Don't worry, Mahcie," he whispers.
"I wanted to."

Like the earth pulling on the moon,
and the moon pulling on the tide,
his lips gravitate
toward mine.

## Kissing J.D.

I feel
like I'm standing
in a rocking canoe.

## Tomorrow, Tomorrow

The only way
I am able to fall asleep
is to promise myself that

I'll straighten everything out
in the morning.

# I Inherited It

I wonder what Dad would say
if I told him that
I liked two boys.
Would he ask me
    if they were cute?

Yes, I'd tell him.

One in a brown-eyed, emo,
Dan Humphrey
kind of way.

The other in a David Beckham
meets Prince Harry
sorta way.

Then I'd ask him how he managed
the ping-ponging feelings
that accompany liking
two people at one time.

Because kissing J.D.
felt amazing one minute
and terrible the next.

## Would He Tell Me?

Would he tell me
that liking two people
wasn't a problem,
but acting on those feelings
was one helluva bad idea?

Would he tell me
that falling out of love
isn't nearly as painful
as admitting it?

Would he tell me
that it would've broken his heart
to tell Mom the truth—
so he chickened out
and didn't tell her?

Would he tell me
that taking a sledgehammer
to the house he built
was the last thing
he wanted to do?

Would he tell me
he loved me *almost*
more than anything,
but not enough
to keep pretending?

# Procrastination

I have done my history assignment,
my geometry proofs,
and an essay for English.

I have cleaned the kitchen,
my bedroom,
and even the toilet.

I have taken out the trash,
the recycling,
and taken a walk.

I haven't called J.D.
or Linus
or even Katie.

I haven't solved my problem.
I haven't told J.D., "It was only a kiss—
    I have a boyfriend.
    I made a mistake."

I haven't told Linus, "I kissed another boy.
    It didn't mean anything,
    but I thought you should know
    I made a mistake."

I haven't IM'd Katie
    because she's friends with Linus
    and my mistake
                would put her smack
                in the middle
                of an awkward situation.

## *Maybe*

Maybe my attraction to J.D.
is just physical.

Or maybe there is too much distance
between Linus and me.

Or maybe all this loneliness
and no security blanket
has messed with my head.

## The End

I know
I need to call Linus
and tell him about J.D.
or at least let him know
that maybe we should see other people,
since
I'm far away

and probably not
coming back.

# I Told My Mother

I told my mother she was
    self-centered
    stubborn
    bitchy
    and
    stuck in a rut.

I told my mother she should
    put on a bra
    see the colors on the trees
    eat lobster at Newick's
    and
    take Dad's Mustang for a drive up the coast.

I told my mother she couldn't
    go on moping about Dad's boyfriend
    sleep all day and all night
    eat only sourdough toast
    and
    pretend that the rest of the world does not exist.

I told my mother that I
    didn't mind chipping in and doing my chores
    but doing all the housework was another story,
    especially
    when my social life was picking up
    and my morals were falling down.

I asked her (in a near-hysterical shriek),
    "Since when am I the parent and you the teenager?"

## *Now*

I feel guilty
for being the big, bad, mean grown-up
when all she needs
is a
friend.

# The Next Best Thing to a Security Blanket

The box springs creak
as I climb into bed with my mother.

My tears dampen her pillow.

She pushes my hair back
and pulls me close.

I sob that
    I am sorry
    I must be a bad person
    if I can't love my own mother
    (or even my boyfriend)
    if I can't understand another person's loss
    and only think of myself.

She shushes me with quiet disagreements, telling me that
    it is wrong
    for an adult to burden a child
    with personal problems
    that are best discussed among adults.

On the other hand, she explains,
    it is okay
    for a child to turn to an adult
    when things get complicated.

And it would be better for both of us
    if she were the mother and
    I were the teenager,
    and if I wanted to talk about things
    she'd be happy to listen.

I decline.
    She doesn't need my problems
    on top of her own.

## Morning

I awake
to the smell of
my mother
making pancakes
with little
round slices
of bananas
fried into them.

## Peeking from Behind My Locker Door

I watch J.D. come down the hall,
saying hello to cheerleaders,
to guys on the soccer team,
and nodding politely to teachers
as if he is the eighth wonder of the world.

His hair is wet, darker than usual,
he's wearing an OR school sweatshirt
over loose, worn jeans, and Adidas
and he looks as appetizing as he did in a tux.

"Mahcie?" he asks, pulling the locker open
so he can see my face. "Doughnut?"

      "No thanks."

"You're mad at me," he says.

      "Nah. I ate breakfast."

"So you're ignoring me?"

"Yeah, kinda," I admit,
        because I had purposely
        not run into him yesterday
        by skipping lunch.

"Look, I'm sorry about the kiss," he says.

    "Don't be. It was nice—more than nice."

"You just looked so beautiful. . . .
All I'm sayin' is that if you don't wanna—
you know—it's okay with me."

    "Yeah, all right. Thanks."

"But you can't say no to coffee."

    "Of course not, you've got me addicted."

## I Take the Cup of Coffee

brushing J.D.'s fingers
before he turns to go.

Anger flashes over me
and I tilt the cup back,
gripping it like a football.

I stop myself
before I throw it at him.

Dammit, I want to shout
why the hell do you
have to be so nice?

You just apologized for kissing me?
Guys don't apologize for things like that.
You're too goddamned perfect.

Stop it.

Before I hate you.

Before I like you
too much.

Stomping into homeroom,
I toss the coffee into the trash can
and swear not to think
about kissing J.D.
ever again.

# My Sweaters Arrive Parcel Post

Snuggled among soft sweaters,
fleece-lined hoodies,
jeans,
and leather boots
are three little boxes.

Not *good* little boxes,
like that hold jewelry,
but logo-emblazoned,
drugstore boxes—
slick and shiny,
and glued shut.

I don't even want
to look at them.

I don't want
to think about them.

I can't believe
my *dad* sent me them!

Because inside the boxes are
individually wrapped condoms:
    1. In a rainbow of neon colors
    2. In latex-free for sensitive skin
    3. In fruity flavors

There's also an envelope
with a letter from Dad.

# I Open the Envelope Dad Sent

Dear Marcie,

I miss you. I hope school is going okay. Everything's all right here, a bit quiet.

I know that we've had this conversation before, but I was thinking about you and your friendship with J.D. Sometimes good friends become more than friends, which is normal because our friends understand us best and we are comfortable around them. That's why I'm sending the condoms. I want you to be prepared if the special moment comes along.

Your mother has encouraged you to wait until marriage, and if that is right for you it is a great decision and I will support it. Then again, I don't want you rushing off to get married the minute you turn eighteen. That isn't a good decision. Instead, think carefully about sex and what is right for you. Always, always protect yourself.

Sex, like alcohol and drugs, can have life-altering consequences. Unlike beer and meth, it can be wonderful and special.

I know you understand that you can get pregnant and if you do, there are options like abortion, adoption, and keeping the baby. Your friend Emily gave her baby up, while Linus's brother and his girlfriend kept theirs. I'm sure you have witnessed the hardships brought on by these decisions.

STDs are the other risks you take. Some are curable, others will change (and maybe shorten) your life. As a father, I don't want any of these things to happen to the daughter I love very much.

Please be careful, very careful. I love you.

Dad

# I Crumple It Up

My father thinks
I'm falling for J.D.?

I'm not.

He's too
perfect.

## Back to the Boxes

To cheer myself up,
I take a neon-green condom from its candy wrapper,
feeling the slippery softness with my fingers.
I tuck it under my pillow,
and sneak to the kitchen for a banana.

Reading the instructions
(and gawking at the pictures)
I roll my lime-green condom
over the perky yellow banana,
which cracks me up
beyond reason.

I howl with laughter
as I dial Katie's number.
Tears squirting from my eyes,
I try to explain how funny it looks.

But all she says is,
"Marcie, why'd your dad
send you condoms?"

## I Explain

about how J.D. looks
like David Beckham in his soccer uniform
but smiles like Prince Harry
with boy-band dimples—
that he's just too goddamned perfect.

"I can't believe you dumped Linus and didn't tell me!"

"I didn't *not* tell you, Katie! I swear!"
She is, after all, my best friend.
And I'd never keep a secret like that from her.

"I haven't dumped Linus.
It was just a birthday kiss,
nothing more.
I don't even like J.D.
I swear."

## Lambasted

Katie
gets
righteous
on my
ass.

Threatening
to tell the sweetest
brown-eyed Leftover
boy
on planet Earth
that
his
long-distance girlfriend
isn't watching
his YouTube videos,
but rather
kissing
another
boy
good night.

## Katie, You Don't Understand

how lonely it is here
without any friends.

My mother is so distant
I need a telescope to see her.

My father is a stranger
whom I no longer know.

My Gigi has gone loopy, old-lady crazy
and tells me to wash my hair with mayonnaise.

My aunt Greta buys me panties
the size of South Dakota.

J.D. is the only person here
who makes any sense.

# It Was Dumb. I Know.

But I got swept up—
J.D. invited me to homecoming.
He wore a tux.
And I, a blue satin prom dress.
It was just like in the movies.

My mother forgot my birthday
and J.D. planned a party,
invited all his friends,
had his sisters make a cake.
It was just like in the movies.

So when he kissed me good night
it felt like part of a script.
I got wrapped up in the plot—
just like watching a good movie.

It was dumb.
I know.

## What Best Friends Are For

Katie seemed to understand
that J.D.'s good looks
and sweet gestures
would be too much
for any girl
to turn
away

and
that if it
was just one kiss—
nothing more than a moment of weakness—
she guessed she could live with the whole idea,
and keep it a secret from Linus. She promised.

"Just one kiss," I repeat. "Because I can't stand
how stupid perfect J.D. can be."

## Trapped

The shades have not been opened,
the dishes have not been washed,
and my mother has not left her bed.

At least when she did this over the summer,
I could sit on the dock, explore the woods and marsh,
soak up some sunshine,
and ignore her.

But here there are four walls,
a bookstore below us,
and another apartment above.

Trapped.

## Home from School (Almost)

Today
I can't bear it.
I can't go inside
that dark,
four-room tomb.

I hang out downstairs
in the bookstore,
sunk on my haunches,
reading college textbooks
among the stacks
with plenty of time
to think.

# Change Is Good

I need a change.
Not an Idaho > New Hampshire kind,
but a change in attitude.

All summer,
I didn't talk much with the townies.
(I thought I was only going to be here
    for a few months.)

But now it's time to be Superman,
find a phone booth,
spin around,
and become a townie.

## I Try Making Friends

I spy Sam sitting alone, her head bent
over Mary Shelley's *Frankenstein*.

"Sam?" I interrupt her reading.
"I was wondering if maybe—"

> "Don't bother," she chops my words off.
> "You want to be popular. I understand.
> And popular kids, like J. D. Gallagher, don't
> like me.
> So don't bother."

I wanted to say that I missed having friends
who were girls, who gossiped and were silly,
and not nearly as boring as the popular girls
who only talked about fashion and horse shows.

"You sure?" I ask instead.

> "I'm sure. I'd only talk trash about the kids you
> sit with, anyway."

"Like what?"

"Like J. D. Gallagher is a serial dater,
Melanie Hanson needs to go to rehab,
and Conner Lakoski has HPV."

"How do you know all this?"

"People talk
when they think no one is listening."

## A Silent Thank-you Note

I have to thank Sam
for making the upper crust
at Oyster River
seem like
Boise High
Leftovers.

But what did she mean by
*serial dater*?

## November 18—11:33 P.M.

| | |
|---|---|
| *MarsBars* | *am i such an awful friend?* |
| EmoK8 | girlfriend, maybe . . . |
| | but friend-friend, no. |
| *MarsBars* | *ouch.* |
| EmoK8 | marcie, it's the truth. |
| *MarsBars* | *ok, ok. it's just that i asked this girl* |
| | *if she wanted to be friends* |
| | *and she said no.* |
| EmoK8 | wtf? |
| *MarsBars* | *not those \*exact\* words, but close enough.* |
| EmoK8 | oh, marcie, that's terrible. |
| | god, you must feel like crap. |
| *MarsBars* | *sorta. crap girlfriend.* |
| | *crap friend.* |
| | *is this crap genetic?* |
| EmoK8 | well, your dad was a crap husband, |
| | even if he's a cool dad. |
| *MarsBars* | *and my mom makes a lousy friend.* |
| | *she \*says\* we can talk, but she already has* |
| | *101 things to be depressed about.* |
| EmoK8 | i'm here. talk to me. |
| *MarsBars* | *i miss that, just hanging out* |

|          |                                        |
|----------|----------------------------------------|
|          | *with our pencils and notebooks.*      |
|          | *i even miss studying at your house.*  |
| EmoK8    | as if we get any studying done         |
|          | with all the Leftovers here.           |
| *MarsBars* | *hmm. i think that's the point.*     |
| EmoK8    | i don't get any studying done          |
|          | with angelo here.                      |
|          | he sends out latin love vibes.         |
| *MarsBars* | *pheromones?*                        |
| EmoK8    | no, more like, on the bright side,     |
|          | i'm now the girlfriend of a sex god.   |
| *MarsBars* | *don't tell me that you've had sex?* |
| EmoK8    | no.                                    |
| *MarsBars* | *phew!*                              |
| EmoK8    | remember the plan?                     |
|          | we're gonna get our                    |
|          | birth control pills together.          |
| *MarsBars* | *like anyone will ever want to have sex w me?* |
| EmoK8    | i'm sure linus will, someday.          |
| *MarsBars* | *i hope so. i'm shriveling up from lack of hugs.* |
| EmoK8    | (------------------☺--------------------) |
| *MarsBars* | *thanx. I luv u.*                    |
| EmoK8    | luv u 2. nite.                         |

## Questions

"Sam," I whisper in the library,
"what did you mean by *serial dater*?"

"Cripes, Mahcie, you like him, don't you?"

"Tell me," I plead.

"I meant
    that if a guy has a body like J. D. Gallagher,
    a face that belongs in a Disney movie,
    combined with his sweet, sincere, Boy Scout personality,
    he can get any girl he wants."

"You didn't answer my question."

"Did I mention J.D. wants everything cute and female?"

"So he dates a lot?"

"If by 'a lot' you mean
    every girl from Maine to Massachusetts?
Yeah."

## Chasing Boys

On Saturday,
J.D. rings my doorbell
    (looking as adorable as ever,
      with his toothpaste-commercial smile,
        messy morning hair, and cheeks pink from the cold)
and greets me with doughnuts and coffee.

I consider not letting him in.
    Ending our friendship
    before it goes anywhere I don't want it to go.
    But he looks so cute, so eager,
    it would be like spanking a puppy for
    bringing you the newspaper.

"Argh," I tell him instead.
    "Now that I live in town,
    I can't eat doughnuts every morning.
I'll get fat."

"You won't if you exercise," he says,
then invites me out for a jog
    (and waits for me to change my clothes
    and find my sneakers under the couch).

He shows me a few key stretches
     (which reveal two cans of his six-pack,
     and the fact that he's wearing Calvin Kleins),
bounds down the flight of stairs,
and hits the pavement at a steady pace.

I keep up with him as we weave through
the coffee shop crowd,
up the hill past the redbrick university,
and out of town,
hitting the highway
     with fire in my lungs
     forgiveness in my head
     and desire in my heart.

# Answering Machine Message from Linus

*Please call me sometime.*
*Katie says things aren't so good.*
*I really miss you.*

I called him back
and choked up
when he told me
how much he
missed
me.

"I miss you too,"
I said back,
crying not
because I did
but because I didn't know
if I was telling the truth.

# Baking Pies for Thanksgiving

My mother doesn't believe in women's work.
She thinks in terms of equality, equal pay.
A second-wave feminist with one little quirk.

She washes her hands, dons apron as if to say,
"To hell with philosophy, religion, and politics,
I am woman! I will make pies today!"

She reveals old secrets, tapioca tricks,
how to slice the apples, stir in sugar and spice,
make pea-sized crumbles and not overmix.

Dust the counter in flour, the rolling pin, twice
from the center out, short strokes for flaky crust
lift the dough carefully, lower slowly, be precise.

Fill the pan high with apples, pride, love, and trust,
weave dough strips in and out for a basket top
and don't forget to dab with milk, it's a must.

With the pie in the hot oven, down she'll flop.
"I did my duty, taught my daughter to bake
and not to buy a pie at the corner shop."

# Thanksgiving at Aunt Greta's

## (DOESN'T COMPARE TO DAD'S COOKING)

Turkey
Baked potatoes
Sweet potatoes
Stuffing
Cranberry sauce
Green beans and almonds
Tossed salad
Apple pie and ice cream
and
Half a glass of white wine.

# Like Clockwork

J.D. shows up at my door
in his sweats and sneakers,
asking if I am too sore for another run.

"No," I say, because my quads
only hurt a little
and being alone all weekend
hurts a lot.

"You know," he says, setting the stride,
"we should hang out more often."

"I've got a gift certificate to the mall in Manchester.
We could go Christmas shopping."

"A road trip?" he asks.

# Blue Cafeteria Trays

must be rare.
I got one today,
sat down next to J.D.,
and everyone
started laughing
and punching J.D. on the shoulder,
as if they knew
we spent all of Saturday
breathing the same air.

When I asked
what was going on,
they said a blue tray
meant you were
going to get laid.

## How I Learned that the Cutest Jock at OR Had a Crush

J.D. picks me up at my locker,
offering me a ride home.

"Why don't we get a slice?" I suggest.

"Yeah, maybe." He sounds distracted,
turns the key in the ignition,
but doesn't back out of the parking space.
"I'm sorry about the blue tray thing."

"Oh, J.D. It's not a big deal."

"I told Conner how much I like you,
and he kinda blabbed it around."

So J. D. Gallagher *does* want me.

"You're pretty and smart, but different.
You don't care that I can't dance.
You didn't laugh at my sisters' cake.

And you talk about everything
but clothes and horses."

       "Thanks."

"What I mean is,
I had a great time this weekend."

       "Me too."

"No hard feelings?"

       "Nope."

"So how about that slice?"

       "Do you like marshmallows?"

"Huh?"

       "I changed my mind."

## S'mores

After a quick stop at the Durham Market
to pick up marshmallows, graham crackers,
and Hershey's Special Dark,
J.D. follows my directions,
turning
    right at the stoplight,
    left at the Y,
    and left down a gravel lane.

With the spare key,
I open the door to the summerhouse,
where we sit cross-legged on the floor
and breathe a fire to life in the potbellied stove.

Waiting for coals,
J.D. asks me about Idaho,
    what it looks like and how much it snows.
I ask him what J.D. stands for
    and if he prefers the nickname
    to the full-blown one like I do.
He asks me about my friends
    and what we do for fun.

I ask him about Conner
    and how long they've known each other.
He asks about Katie
    and if I like manga, too.

We toast marshmallows on barbecue skewers,

        sandwich the molten sugar
    between two crackers and a square of chocolate,
        and eat them in slow motion
            to savor the sweetness.

# I Don't Know Who Started It

It may have been me
reaching to wipe chocolate
from the corner of his mouth.

It may have been him
kissing marshmallow goo
from my sticky sweet fingers.

It might have been me
wondering if his lips were sweeter
than marshmallows and chocolate.

It might have been him
wondering what it'd feel like
to touch the skin under my shirt.

All I know is
chocolate and marshmallows
weren't the only things melting
in the heat of the coals.

## Writer's Block

I'm writing Linus an email
to make us
just friends.

But it's so mean
(to dump him via email).

I can't hit Send.

## J.D. and I

share secret smiles
over Styrofoam cups of hot coffee,
in the halls between classes,
over ordinary cafeteria trays,
when Conner isn't watching.

# News to Me

Friday night, J.D. and I
and some other kids
snuck into a frat party.

I thought they'd kick us out
because we weren't college students,
but J.D. said the Greeks were open
to showing everyone a good time.

Inside the floor pulsed with bass.
The sound waves made me seasick
as they rolled through my body.
I liked the woozy feeling
because I could act tipsy
while drinking Diet Coke.

Because J.D. doesn't dance,
I was nestled deep within his embrace,
swaying to the music

when some girl shrieked,
"YOU'RE DANCING WITH MY BOYFRIEND!"

## In the Aftermath of Operation Girlfriend Defreak

J.D. brings me
two jelly doughnuts
and a large cuppa Dunkin'
on Saturday morning.

"Maybe I should have told you
I had a sorta girlfriend."

  "No biggie.
  I have a boyfriend."

"Huh?"

### 3.1 *Miles of Conversation*

J.D. and I have so much to explain
to each other,
to ourselves,

that our jog takes us
all the way
to the summerhouse

before
we begin to understand
each other,
ourselves.

## *Megan*

"She lives in the North Country,"
he tells me,
as if northern New Hampshire
is a territory yet to be accepted
into the union.

"We met over the summer,
where we worked as junior counselors
at a soccer summer camp.
It should have been a summer fling,
but because we had sex,
I couldn't bring myself to
break it off.

No official end.
No official 'let's be friends.'

So, technically,
she's still my girlfriend."

## Telling Truths

"Linus and I," I explain,
"have been friends since junior high
and more-than-friends since April.

I've been meaning to ask him
if we can go back to being just friends.

But, he's kinda emo-sensitive,
and I know it'd really crush him."

J.D. and I sit on the rocks
and watch the tide recede.

I admit into the silence
that I don't really know
what to do about
my relationship with Linus,
because it isn't all chocolate-covered strawberries dipped
in whipped cream
and there certainly weren't any misplaced back rubs.

## Nickname

"Linus?" J.D. asks.

I tell J.D. about
Linus's three older brothers
and how they picked on him
without mercy,
christening him
with the name
of the *Peanuts* character
he most resembled
when he was four.

## Opportunity Knocks

J.D. and I share more secrets
as we warm our aching muscles
in front of the potbellied stove.

He had sex with Megan three times.
Me and Linus none at all.

"Never?" he asks.

      "Nope."

"You wanted to?"

      "Yeah."

Upon hearing this, J.D. takes his shirt off
and tells me that I can do whatever I want.

Except all I can think of
is his poor, unglued girlfriend
who had sex
three times.

## Overactive Imagination

But that night, alone in bed
I let my dream fingers
trace every muscle—
each rise and valley—
on J.D.'s beautiful torso.

I let my dream eyes
connect the dots between the freckles
that spill over his shoulders
as if he stood in pink lemonade rain.

I can almost taste
his hard-earned sweat
salty and masculine
on my dream tongue.

## Kissing as a Recreational Sport

After J.D. and I
firmly establish
that we are otherwise engaged,
we find ourselves
sequestered in the summerhouse
every afternoon after school,
building little fires,
and kissing until our lips are chapped
and my face has rug burns
from the stubble on his chin.

# Answering Machine Message from Dad

*Charlene, I got your message.*
*Sorry my phone was off. I was at work.*
*Yes, we can talk about Marcie.*

Mom calls Dad back
late at night.

And since we only have one phone
I can't listen in on the other line.

Her voice is quiet.
And I can't quite hear
what she is telling him
about me.

## Because I Love Her

Ignoring my mother
isn't helping.

Even when I'm not there,

> where I can't see
> her sad tired eyes
> her thin petite frame
> her messy curly hair

> where I can't smell
> her toast
> her coffee
> her unwashed blankets

> where I can't hear
> her snores
> her fingers tapping the keyboard
> her silence

> where I can't feel
> her cool hand in mine

her warm embrace
her pain

I still remember.

## *Memory*

Thinking back,
I remember a time or two,
(maybe three)
when Mommy shut herself
into the bedroom.

Daddy would tell me to play quietly.
"Sh," he'd say. "Mommy's sleeping."

But he'd let me help make her toast
and fresh-squeezed orange juice.

We'd make up a tray
(just like for breakfast in bed)
even though it was
the middle of the afternoon.

And Daddy would always put
two pills in a little bowl
next to the glass of orange juice.

We'd sit on the bed
in the darkened room,
quiet while Mommy

tried to smile.

## Illness

It helps if I imagine
that depression is like the flu,
or if I pretend that she has cramps
and can't possibly get out of bed.

I bring her orange juice,
chicken noodle soup,
One A Day vitamins.

I tell her about my day,
my grades in biology,
that Gigi had called.

I give her every opportunity
to tell me what she is telling Dad,
but she remains silent.

I bundle her up in G'pa's bomber jacket
and take her to the deli for pitas,
to Wildcat's for pizza,
and to the sit-down place for salad.

I wait for her to sip her coffee,
to finish her food,
to thank me and smile.

## At the Bagel Shop

I drag Mom out for breakfast
at one in the afternoon
while our clothes spin dry.

J.D. comes in with two guys from school
and wearing a mint-green T-shirt,
looking as edible as ice cream.

They must have ordered soup
because their table is piled deep
with packages of crackers.

I steal glances his way,
watching him make a saltine and cream cheese sandwich
and put the whole thing in his mouth.

I flush pink when he smiles at me
even though he has gooey white stuff
stuck in his teeth.

## At the Laundromat

Mom pulls warm, fluffy clothes from the dryer,
trailing socks and unmentionables across the tiles.

I play sweeper picking them up.

"You missed one,"
J.D. says from behind me.
Dangling from his index finger

                    is a pair of very tiny
                        black lace
                          panties.

I snatch them away,
but at the same time
I realize
they aren't mine.

In fact, there is a Victoria's Secret

                    price tag
                    dangling
                    from the
                    dark lace.

## Change of Season

J.D. drags me out
on a run, promising me
pine trees and snowflakes.

"Underpants?
You gave me underpants?"
I curse J.D.

He laughs.
He runs faster.

"That's, like, so not appropriate!"
I chase him down.

He stops.
Hands on his knees, he gasps between laughs,
telling me they were my Christmas present.

"Not funny. My mom was there!"

"Come on, Mahcie, I can see your granny panties,
every time you touch your toes."

I whack him one on the shoulder.

"So I just thought . . ." he trails off.

"You didn't think
I'd show them to you . . . on.
Did you?"

He just grins
big.

# Friends with Benefits

Long after the cool sunlight has sunk below the trees,
after the darkness has seeped in through the cracks in
    the summerhouse walls,
after our fire has dimmed to highlighter-orange coals,

J.D. slides behind me,
making a chair out of his knees,
a headrest out of his chest.

He wriggles from his sweatshirt,
then lifts mine off over my head,
kissing the back of my neck,
the muscles of my shoulders,
until tingles make me giggle.

I turn and kiss him,
his warm soft lips,
his pressing mouth,
pretending not to notice
the freeing spring
of my bra
coming
undone.

## Thank God

Finally!
My second bases
have been rounded.

I was beginning to think
that there was something wrong
with them/with me.

Because, no boy
(not one single horny-assed teenage boy)
paid my breasts any attention

until now.

## My Mother Is Wrong

about so many things.

Lingerie makes a great gift not an inappropriate one.
I should know. I own two pieces.
    A camisole from Katie.
    A pair of little black lace panties from J.D.
And when I put them on under my clothes I feel
    soft and silky like I just took a shower
    mysterious like I know a secret no one else does
    sexy like I want to kiss J.D. passionately
        for the next forty-five minutes.

Standing up for myself would be so boring.
I should know. I let J.D. touch me. A lot.
    Above my knee under the cafeteria table.
    Under my shirt in front of the potbellied stove.
And when he puts his hands under my clothes I feel
    beautiful like a girl on the cover of a glossy magazine
    desired like a tall glass of lemonade on a hot July
        afternoon
    sexy like I want to kiss him passionately
        for the next forty-five minutes.

Hating men isn't better than loving them.
I should know. I have been *almost* in love more than once.
> With Linus Thomas.
> With Jeremiah Delaney Gallagher.
And when I am with a guy I like I feel
> special like a box of chocolates on Valentine's Day
> valued like a string of pearls
> sexy like I want to kiss him passionately
>> for the next forty-five minutes.


Hiding in bed all day isn't better than living my life.
I should know. I tried it.
> I had my covers up to my chin.
> And my pillow over my head.
But when J.D. knocked on the door this morning I felt
> my heart jump like I just heard a crack of lightning
> my pulse pound like I just ran from here to the
>> summerhouse
> my breath quicken like I had been kissing J.D.
>> for the last forty-five minutes.

# Overheard

When I came in all sweaty and needing a shower,
I heard my mother say,
　　"I've got to go. Marcie's home from her run,"
　　and she hurried to hang up the phone.

All I could think about while I washed my hair
　　was that she didn't sound pleased.

I have a feeling that my mother doesn't like J.D.
　　(Because she can't possibly not like my jogging.)

# J.D. Knows to Avoid the Potholes

and how to ease his Jeep
down the dark gravel lane
without making a sound.

He flashes me a grin in the dashboard light
that means he'd love to warm his hands
on the skin under my shirt.

He slams on the brakes.
My seat belt tugs me back to present tense.

"A deer?"

     "No, look!"

I follow the high beams,
expecting a bear, or maybe a moose
or even a loose buffalo from the farm down the street.
Just about anything
but a Mustang

and my father.

## *"Hi, Daddy!"*

I say as if I'm happy to see him
as if he isn't interrupting anything
by parking his car,
and himself,
in the middle of the lane.

"Marcie,
how come your mother knew
that I'd find you here?"

"'Cause one of the neighbors called and said
that the kitchen window had come open
so J.D. and I thought we'd check on it?" I lie.

"So you have a key?"

"Huh?"

Dad takes my hand,
emptying it of its key-ring contents.
He inspects the keys by the headlights.
And I can tell that he recognizes the worn brass gem

that has been opening the door to the summerhouse
since 1954.

> "I'm sorry, J.D.,
> but Marcie and I have a little catching up to do.
> Would you mind giving us a moment?"

> "No prob, Mistah Fostah.
> It was nice to meet you.
> 'Night, Mahcie."

"'Night," I say.
But scream in my head,
Don't leave me!

Dad will start in on one of his
heart-to-heart conversations
about good friends, sex, and prophylactics.

# My Father Wraps Me in His Long Arms

His fine wool sweater is
soft and warm on my cheek.
He smells like leather and cedar
and reminds me of home.

"I've missed you, Sugar Cookie."

I try to tell him that I missed him too,
but sobs choke in my throat.

It feels so good to hug him,
I don't want to let go.
I hug him tighter.

He pulls me closer
and wonders in a half whisper,
"Maybe I should have come
to get you sooner."

## Dad Doesn't Lecture Me

He just asks
if I know what
Mom's family meeting
is about.

## Back at Our Apartment

I treat my father like a guest,
pouring him a glass of wine
because we don't have gin.

"So, Charlene, you wanted to talk face-to-face?"
he asks Mom, looking cool and comfortable
while she paces and sweats.

"I—I—I found these in Marcie's room!"
From her pocket, Mom pulls out
a stack of
condom
packages
that unfold
like an
accordion.

"Yeah," Dad says.
"I gave them to her."

"Ethan! What the hell were you thinking?"

"That I wasn't going to count on
some seventeen-year-old jock
to remember them."

"But she's just a kid!"

"She's sixteen, Charlene.
There's nothing wrong
with giving her a parachute."

Mom puts her hands over her ears,
and stomps back and forth in mad
half circles around the coffee table.

"Mom?"
"MOM?"
"MOM, STOP!"

She stops pacing and looks at me.

"I didn't use them.
I mean,
I put one on a banana.
Just to practice.

But J.D. and I
don't have sex.
And I've never slept
with Linus.
I mean,
we've slept together,
but we just slept.
With our clothes on."

"See!" Mom shouts at Dad.
"You're encouraging her!
I can't deal with this.
I just can't deal with this. . . ."

## Funny

but when Mom
has one of her
breakdowns

the only person
who can glue the pieces
together again

is still Daddy.

## In the Aftermath of Operation Sedate My Mother

In the morning,
my father
takes me out
for doughnuts,
which we eat
on the porch
of the summerhouse,
our coffee cups
and our breath
steaming.

"Your mom and I
decided
it would be best
if you
came back to Boise,
with me."

## Protesting

"But Mom needs me!"

      "Marcie," he says, "she'll be all right."

"No, Daddy, you don't know how it is.
Mom *needs* me."

I plunk my coffee cup on the railing,
stomp down the steps.
"You weren't here,
you wouldn't know," I tell him
over my shoulder as
I make my escape.

"She needs me.
She needs me."

I chant as I jog,
finding my pace
and enjoying

the crunch of snow
under my sneakers.

"She needs me.
She needs me."

## Escort

Dad
drives
real
slow
on
the
pavement
behind
me.
"Marcie?"
"Sugar Cookie?"
"Please?"

I fall
into a
rhythm
down
Durham
Point
Road
that
takes
me
into
town.

## How I Got to the Bottom of Things

Lungs burning,
thighs screaming,
and chest heaving,
I stumble up the steps
to our apartment.

Mom looks up from her coffee. "Marcie, honey?"

"Dad says I need to go.
That's not right,

right?

It's not true,

is it?"

"Sweetie," she says, dropping her voice,
like she's saying it's true
without speaking the words.

"You need me to
run to the market
and buy groceries."

"I don't need you
sneaking into the summerhouse
to make out with your boyfriend."

"You need me to
save quarters
and wash our clothes."

"I don't need you
not coming home
right after school."

"You need me to
wash your coffee mugs
and clean the counters."

"I don't need you
acting like
some child I didn't raise."

"You need me. . . ."

"I don't need to worry
about you."

## Realization

I collapse
in a
hardly breathing
sweaty mess
on the couch,
hiccuping tears
into the pillows

and realize
that
she doesn't
need me.

In fact,
she doesn't even
*want* me.

MarsBars: *good news.*

EmoK8: you got straight As?

MarsBars: *nope. im coming home.*

EmoK8: whoopeeeeee! *dances around the room*

MarsBars: *i can't wait to see u!*

EmoK8: so your mom changed her mind?

MarsBars: *about me.*
*she found the condoms.*
*she's shipping me home with dad.*

EmoK8: omg! is she mad?

MarsBars: *yeah. big time.*

EmoK8: but you didnt use the condoms.

MarsBars: *no. but she didnt believe me.*

EmoK8: figures. but at least ur coming home.

MarsBars: *i dont know when we'll get there.*
*we're driving.*

EmoK8: drive safe. i want my BFF in one piece.

MarsBars: *ok*

EmoK8: can i tell the leftovers?

MarsBars: *yeah, sure*

EmoK8: see u soon. luv u. nite.

MarsBars: *nite.*

## *My Good-byes*

to Sam, Conner,
and the popular girls
are short and sweet
on the day before
Christmas break.

I return my textbooks,
my combination lock.

I empty my locker
into a box.

I kiss J.D.
quickly
and hug him
innocently

because my dad
is standing
behind us.

## Holidaze

I am in no mood for Christmas.
How can I celebrate this morning
when I was up all night listening to
my parents talk about getting a divorce?

Dad was begging Mom not to
because the courts wouldn't look at him too favorably.
And he doesn't want to lose me.

He offered her health insurance, rent, and a car
in exchange for me.

He promised not to get married again,
and that he'd sign the papers if she wanted to remarry.

She said that she didn't need
his health insurance,
his money,
his car,

or his permission.

## Christmas Dinner

I think it's a conspiracy,
Mom and Dad against me.

(They have driven me to Manchester,
where I can't possibly sneak out
to devour J.D.)

Until
Arthur insists that Dad carve the turkey.
Dad accepts, not wanting to be rude.
But my mother protests under her breath,
so low only Greta and Grammie Iris can hear.

Grammie Iris gives my mother
a disapproving glance
as if Mom
were still

a child.

## Comfort

Gigi and I take a nap
on Arthur's bed
just to get away from it all.

"Mahcie?" she says
 when I think she is asleep.
"I know it's hard to imagine,
 but they'll figure things out."

             "Thanks, Gigi," I say.

"Your G'pa and I had our moments,
 but we always did what was best
 for our children.

That's what parents do."

## Back to Bed

I sneak out for a run
before Mom wakes up.
(Dad has a hotel room.)

Taking the route around Mill Pond
and up Faculty Row,
I tap-tap on J.D.'s door
instead of ringing the bell.

"He's sleeping," his littlest sister tells me.
"And I'm *not* waking him up."

She lets me in anyway,
as if she plans on summoning
someone else to interrupt her brother's slumber.

Tiptoeing up the stairs,
she beckons me to follow.
At the top she opens a bedroom door.
"You do it," she says.

In the slanted polygons of morning light
that edge their way around the blinds,

J.D. sleeps on his stomach.
His face is smooshed into the pillow.
And he doesn't look like the grizzly bear
his sister had imagined.

"Morning," I say.               "Mmph?"

"Wanna go for a run?"           "Nah," he says,
                                  rolling on his side
                                  and patting the mattress.

I sit on the bed.               He shakes his head.
                                "Lie down."

I ease off my sneakers.
J.D. lifts the covers and
wraps them over me
leaving his arms
in the embrace.                 "That's bettah,"
                                  he mumbles into my hair.
                                "Now sleep."

## In Bed

I fell asleep
wrapped in J.D.'s blankets
wrapped in J.D.'s embrace
wrapped in J.D.'s sleepy warmth

I awoke
tangled in flannel sheets
tangled in J.D.'s arms
tangled in my dreams.

Blinking the room into focus,
I watch J.D. watch me.      "I've never woken up
with a girl in my bed,"
he says through a smile.

But his gaze clouds over
and his smile inverts to a pout.
"I thought you were leaving."

## *"I Am."*

"Because Mom doesn't want me,
 and Daddy wants me home."

        "I want you."

"J.D.," I whine,
"don't make this harder than it already is."

        With that he giggles
        and buries his face in the pillow.

"It's not funny. It's sad," I insist.

        His ears turn pink as he gasps for air.

"You want something to laugh about?
I'll give you something to laugh about!"

        He shakes his head.

I wiggle my fingers
under his arms and tickle.

J.D. rolls on his side,
frees his arms,
and reaches for me.

I shriek as his tickles dig at my ribs.
I wrestle for a grip on his wrists,
pushing his back flat to the mattress.

*"Not* funny."

"Okay, okay, but just so you know,
next time you crawl into bed with some guy,
don't expect him *not* to wake up with a hard-on."

It's my turn to giggle and blush.
I punch his shoulder.
"I was talking about leaving
being, uh—difficult.
*Not* what's going on in your pants."

"I'll miss you, too, Mahcie."

## *Time Well Wasted*

That's how we spent the day

drizzling sarcasm over the truth
dropping bad jokes like f-bombs

dabbing smiles over sad silences
dribbling giggles into quiet corners

dusting each other's lips with breezy kisses
dripping good-bye tears into Little Bay.

## But Before I Left

J.D. and I had a serious conversation.

"Neither you nor I are good
at long-distance relationships," I said.

    "Because of me and Megan?" he asks.

"And Linus and me."

    "So you want to break up?"

"I don't *want* to.
I just know this won't work.
I'll get lonely. I'll miss you."

    "And you'd wonder if I met someone,"
      J.D. said.

"Oh, I know you'd meet someone.
And you'd say, 'Let's be just friends.'"

    "And she'd have these baby-blue eyes,
      short dark hair, and a cute backside."

"You'd kiss her and say you're sorry."

"Her big panties would drive me crazy."

"You'd kiss her again. I know you would."

"Yeah," he sighed.
"I'm not good at the long-distance thing."

"Me neither."

## Mom's New Car

When I get home,
Mom takes me outside
to show me a Subaru Outback
parked in our space behind the apartment.

She unlocks the doors,
turns the key in the ignition.
"Heated seats," she says,
sounding like she wants me to say something.

(I want to ask about her old car back in Boise
and if I can drive it when I get my license.)

"It's nice," I say instead.
"And it'll be good in the snow."

This car is all Mom.
Practical.
Understated.

And so not Daddy.

## Lobstah Feed

Dad and Mom don't tell the Grapes
exactly why
I'm leaving.

We just enjoy lobsters at Newick's
as if it were the Fourth of July
instead of the evening after Christmas.

Mom wrestles her crustacean
into submission,
refusing any assistance
from Dad

while Greta brags that her lobster pie
is already out of the shell.

Arthur cracks Gigi's claws,
and Gigi gives me the best pieces,
to convince me that
I need to like lobster more than I do
if I want to be a New Englander
after all.

## *MapQuest Says*

It will take forty-one hours and thirteen minutes
to drive Dad's Mustang home. (Mom drove it in four
days, back in June.)

> New Hampshire (I don't want to leave.)
> Massachusetts (I can't tell Dad.)
> New York (Because I don't want Dad to
>     think I don't love him.)
> Pennsylvania (I do.)
> Ohio (But I miss J.D.)
> Indiana (I buy J.D. a postcard in Gary.)
> Illinois (It takes me all the way to La Salle to
>     decide what to write.)
> Iowa (I miss Mom, too.)
> Nebraska ("I love you," she says when I call
>     from Lincoln.)
> Wyoming ("I'm sorry I was so much trouble,"
>     I admit from Cheyenne.)
> Utah ("I'm proud of you," Dad says.)
> Idaho ("This won't be an easy adjustment,
>     but I know you can do it.")

Dad doesn't want to risk getting stuck in the snow
so he listens to the weather report
as if it were the gospel,
and only drives
      when the roads have been cleared,
      the visibility is decent,
      and the flurries light.

It takes us all week.

*part two*

BOISE, IDAHO

## Danny

Our drive from Ogden to Boise
takes all day because of the snow.
I'm tired and looking forward to sleeping in my own bed
for the first time in seven months.

Seeing my house with its little yard,
blue shutters, and yellow glow of a lamp left on
fills me with familiar comfort, like a dream. Only better.

Stepping into the family room, I close my eyes and inhale
the sweet scent of home: maple syrup, cinnamon candles,
and Downy dryer sheets.
It smells like a dream. Only better.

Opening my eyes,
I see a boyish man with an Abercrombie body,
a kind smile, and robin's-egg blue eyes,
wearing nothing but pajama bottoms,
who looks like a dream. Only better.

I jump backward and nearly yelp when
I realize I'm not asleep and he is talking to me.

"Sorry, Marcie, I didn't mean to scare you."

He knows my name.
I squint at him.
He looks a little older than UNH frat boys, but not much.

"Marcie, you've met Danny?" Dad says.

"The boyfr— the bartender, yes."

I just didn't remember him being so
cute.

## Home, in Daylight

My house feels familiar, but oddly different.
I wander from room to room, taking inventory:

There are more gadgets in the kitchen,
  including an espresso machine.

There are more books on the shelves,
  including Ayn Rand novels.

There's an electric razor on the bathroom sink,
  next to Dad's regular one.

There's another car in the garage,
  a baby-blue 1969 Pontiac GTO.
  (Mom's old car is parked outside.)

There is nothing different about Dad and Mom's room,
  except Dad has moved
  into the guest room with Danny
  and Mom isn't here.

At least I have my security blanket,
     pancake mix, and maple syrup,
     to make me feel better about

     coming home.

## I Don't Call Linus

or Katie
on the day before school starts.

I am too humiliated
to admit
that I
dumped my boyfriend
and never
bothered
to
inform
him.

# Dad Gives Me a Ride to School

I step out of Danny's gleaming
baby-blue Pontiac GTO
in my leather boots and an old denim skirt
topped with a soft gray sweater.
My short-cropped hair
accessorized with a little clip.
My features accented with mascara
and minty Burt's Bees lip gloss.

(It's so nice to have a closet full of clothes
and a vanity drawer full of makeup.)

With registration papers
and immunization record
in hand,
I should have been ready
for my first day of school.

But
I'm not.

## *Hello*

Linus isn't ready for the girl
who smiles at him
with Burt's Bees minty lips
because he thinks
I'm someone else.

I am.

## All He Says

"God, you look hot,"
Linus whispers,
wrapping both hands around my head
and kissing my lips so hard
I can't speak
or kiss back.

Softening,
he releases the pressure,
kisses my top lip,
and runs his tongue along the ticklish line
where my lip stops and my mouth begins.

If I had planned to protest,
I no longer could.
I gasp for air
as a wave of tingles surfs down my spine.

Eyes closed tight,
we dive, together,
into a dizzying sea
of kisses.

Underwater
I can't hear a single sound in the hall.
As if everyone has stopped to watch
me drown.

## He Stops Kissing Me

when Katie bounces down the hall,
tackles us, spins us around,
and sings, "Marcie, Marcie, Marcie!"

"I missed you," I tell her ear
as I wrap her in a bear embrace
that dances with happiness.

"I can't wait to catch up,
to show you my drawings
and the manga I'm writing.
You'll help me with the words,
won't you, Marcie?"

"Yes," I tell her,
because I want to spend
every waking moment

together.

# Eating Lunch with the Leftovers

Linus is humming a lullaby, scrawling lyrics on a napkin.
Katie is wearing a prom dress over jeans and Converse.
Angelo is tutoring Katie in math
    and looking down her dress.
Emily is buttoning a flannel shirt over her perfect figure.
Olive is sewing Girl Scout badges to a vest.
Carolina is dipping the tines of her fork into vinegar
    then into her salad.
Garrett is telling Ian about riding his bicycle
    to Lake Lowell,
and Ian is drumming his responses in Morse code.

Our lunch table is so weird,
and at the same time, so normal,
that I am overcome with sappy,
made-for-TV nostalgia
and announce,
"I missed you guys!
I'm glad to be back."
Amid the hugs and high fives,
I'm happy
I have friends
like the Leftovers.

## Silly Hamlet

You don't decide
to be or not to be.

Social suicide is not a question.
(At least not in a world divided
by cafeteria tables
and after-school activities.)

Because
just like that—
with Linus's kiss,
Katie's hug,
and lunch with my friends—

I had become a Leftover
all over

again.

## Dress Rehearsal

My school day is a blur
of lectures without beginnings,
novels I have not read,
math problems I can't solve,
and quizzes I have no answers for.

Instead of listening reading computing answering,
I walk through scenarios
in which I tell Linus about J.D.:

"I really liked him," I'd explain.
"I really needed a friend," I'd say.
"Yeah, it got a little out of control,"
  I'd soften the blow. "I kissed him."
"But J.D. and I said good-bye.
  He had a girlfriend and I have you."
"I won't see him again," I'd promise.

"So if you aren't gay," I'd say gently,
"and if you like me like I like you,
  we should give our relationship
  another try,

time to preheat,
simmer,
bake."
        I'd explain
        because I owe it to him,
        because I've been a crap girlfriend,
        because,
after That Kiss,
I want to kiss him

again.

## The Best-Laid Plans

(FALL OUT THE WINDOW)

After Linus puts
his niece down for a nap,
he and I are alone.
Finally.

I am sweating jittery nervous.
I ask rapid-fire questions.
I put him on the stand.

"Do you think I'm pretty?"          "Oh yeah," Linus
                                       says, low and slow.

"Was I before I lost weight?"       "Uh-huh."

"But you—
How come—
How come you never—

Never once
took my clothes off?"               "Huh?"

"Did you think I was fat?"   "No."

"Ugly?"   "No."

"Then what?"   "I—" he stammers.
"Marcie, I—
  I love you."

## *My World Shatters*

Knowing that
Linus loves me
changes everything.

Except
what I have done.

## Respect

"I never once
 took off your clothes,"
Linus says,
 sliding closer,
 wiping tears
 from my cheeks,

"because
 I didn't want
 to treat you
 like my brothers would."

## Clarification

"So
you're
not
gay?"

"I get a boner every time we French-kiss."

# Confession

"I was so lonely,"
I tell Linus.
"I hadn't made any friends
all summer, because
I thought Mom and I
were coming back in September.
So the kids thought
I was kinda stuck-up,
not talking to them
because they were townies.

But there was this boy.
He brought me doughnuts.
He took me to a dance.
He hugged me—
that's all I wanted.
I wanted someone to hold me
because I was shriveling up
from a lack of hugs.

He touched me—
the hem of my skirt.

And all of a sudden,
I felt beautiful.
I felt wanted.
I felt like a ripe peach

he wanted to devour."

## A Million

*I'm sorry*s
do not make
Linus
stop crying.

# In the Aftermath of the End of the World

I let myself out,
walk home
shaking
and confused.

## In Burst

I throw the front door open
and slam it shut behind me.

"Hey, Sugar Cookie," Dad calls from the kitchen.

    "Don't *Sugar Cookie* me," I shout,
      dropping my backpack to the floor.

Dad looks up from his marinara sauce.

    "This—this is all your fault."
     I rip my arms from my parka sleeves.
    "Did you know my life is a bucket of shit?

    No. A bucket is too small.
    A garbage can,
    a truckload,
    a landfill!"

I start to blubber,
my tears falling on the linoleum
like drops of water off fresh-washed dishes.

# Dad Tries to Hug Me

But I turn my shoulders, shake him off.

"How could you?" I choke out.
"How could you leave Mom?
How could you break us up beyond repair?"

Dad turns the burner down,
then takes a seat at the breakfast bar,
leaving a stool empty for me.

"Marcie, I'm sorry."

"Sorry is for dropping a fork," I inform him,
"for spilling milk—"

He cuts me off. "Your mom and I have drifted apart.
But you need to know that
at one time we were very, very close.
We were a family, with a baby."

"Me?" I ask, softening.

"Yes, you. Sit."

I wipe my nose on a dish towel.

"Charlene used to throw her all into everything she did.
She was a great mom, a copywriter at a huge ad agency,
and she still found time to write novels at night."

"My mom?" I ask.

"She loved it. Loved it all.
But she no longer had time
for our relationship.

Marcie, your mother and I
hadn't been intimate for a long time—
years.

And I don't know if you understand,
but that makes for a lonely existence."

## Why We Did What We Did

I can't believe
he doesn't think
I understand.

I do.

Your arms ache to hold someone—
    you move in slow motion from one hug to the next
    so you won't jostle the warm feeling off your shoulders
    before the next hug comes your way.

Your heart feels hollow—
    that emptiness screams like an addiction to be filled
    even if it means doing hurtful, selfish things
    to get a fix.

"I understand,"
I tell him. "Because
I've been lonely, too."

## Dad's Lecture, Part 2

"It was then,
about two years ago,
that I started treating myself to a martini,
instead of coming home to Charlene.

Because I no longer had a wife I could talk to,
I began sharing my problems with Danny.
First we'd talk over drinks,
    later, over lunch
    or games of racquetball.

It took a while
for me to realize
that I had a deeper friendship with Danny
than I had with Charlene.

So yes, Marcie, this whole situation,
your shit-landfill life,
is all my fault."

## Boiled Down

"So you broke our family
into a million little pieces
for *sex*?"

"For love, Marcie.
That's what families are:
  two people who fall in love,
  make love,
  and give birth to a child they love."

## One More Question

"Before you married Mom,
  did you know you were gay?"

Dad nods.

"Not gay. Bisexual.
I was never able
to put hetero or homo
in front of sexuality.

   I loved Charlene
   and I wanted
   to become a father.

So I tucked
that other part

away."

## Staying Home from School Because My Head Hurts

Dad makes me chamomile tea
and tucks me into bed on the couch
like I am nine and home from school
with a stomachache.

I tell him that nothing
will make me feel better.

Orange juice,
chicken noodle soup,
and One A Day vitamins
won't cure my heartache.

Staying home from school,
and drinking tea on the couch
with my security blanket
won't change the fact
that Linus and I are history.

And J.D. and Mom
are over two thousand miles away.

Dad says,
"Time and love
cure everything."

# I Call Mom

After I blubber about
Linus saying "I love you,"
and my dismal but honest confession,
I tell Mom I'm lonely,
that the house is too big.
That without someone to take care of,
I feel lost.

She says it's too quiet,
that the college kids are at class,
that she wandered around the bookstore today,
because there was no one to talk to.

I tell her I'm sorry
for acting like a teenager,
for not following her advice.

She says she's sorry,
for not being a better mother,
for not taking my advice.

I say that I'll go for a run,
clear my head
if she'll take a walk,
breathe in fresh air.

## After a Loop around the Park

I look at the clock,
add two hours,
and figure J.D. should be
home from school
by now.

I giggle when I hear
him say my name
without all the letters.

"That good?" he asks.

"Say it again."

"What, Mahcie?
I said I pahked the cah
down at Bah Hahbah."

"You paRked the caR
down at BaR HaRboR?"

"I miss you, Mahcie—
even though you talk funny."

I tell him that
I miss him too.

### Innocent Questions

I sit with the Leftovers at lunch,
leaving an empty chair between
myself and Linus.

Everyone is quiet, even Garrett and Ian.
And Katie and Angelo are too wrapped up
in each other to say hello.

"Where were you two lovebirds yesterday?"
Emily inquires, breaking the silence.

> Linus pushes his cafeteria tray away
> as if the thought of me repulses him.

I didn't know that he stayed home yesterday, too,
as if heartbreak were a disease.

> "We broke up," Linus says.

Emily looks at me to verify.

"We did?" I ask him,
unsure of what really happened between
the tears and the truth.

  "Last I checked,
    when your girlfriend cheats on you,
    it's over!"

"Last I checked,
some guys actually touch their girlfriends!"

  "Forgive me for showing you a little respect."

"I didn't want respect," I tell him, sharp and loud.
"I wanted—" I search my brain for the right word.
"I wanted passion!"

## *I Can't Believe*

I once thought
breaking up with Linus
over email
was the worst thing
in the world.

It wasn't.

The way
he looked at me
when we passed
each other
in the hall
before Spanish class

made me feel
guilty sorry miserable
times
a billion.

# I'm So Stupid

Linus had every right to dump me.
And zero reasons to take me back.

Why did I ever think
our relationship deserved
a second chance?

There is no three-strikes
when it comes to dating.
One heartbreak and that's it.

Done.
Over.
Gone.

I really should have told Linus
that I'd rather be just friends,
instead of spilling the goddamned truth.

Katie's right.
I am a crap girlfriend.

Oh my God!
I don't even like

myself.

## A Recipe

"Hey," Katie says,
running to catch up with me.

"Hi." I pretend not to notice her panting.

"You weren't on the bus," she says.
"I saw you walking and got off."

"I didn't feel like seeing Linus."

She's quiet for a few strides, then says,
"You knew this would happen—
that'd he break up with you."

"He said he loved me," I admit.
"So I wasn't sure."

"Whoa, he said, 'I love you'?"

"And then I told him about J.D.
It was horrible."

"And you didn't call me?" Katie asks.

"I felt like shit," I say. "And you were right.
I am a crap girlfriend."

"I'm your best friend! And I didn't know
you broke up with your boyfriend
for two whole days!"

"I didn't want to talk about it."
I don't tell Katie I didn't want to talk to her
because I was ashamed. And she was right.

"I thought you were out sick.
I got your homework assignments."

"Thanks."

Katie shrugs.

We walk a block in silence.

"I can't believe you brought it up at lunch—
the whole cafeteria heard you shouting."

"Emily brought it up."

"She didn't bring up sex and whatnot."

"Passion."

"Passion," Katie says slowly
like she's mulling it over.
"God, Marcie, you're picky."

Katie's words feel like gravel
inside my sneakers.
"You don't understand."

"Then tell me."

"You know that feeling—
the one that says, 'I want sex'?
Passion is more than that.
Love, conversation, understanding,
and the physical stuff—
all stirred together."

"And you have passion cake?" she asks.

"Yeah. That's what I want."

## To Cheer Me Up

Katie says we're having a sleepover,
come hell or high water.
She already told Olive, Carolina, and Em.

I volunteer my house,
because I don't want to go anywhere else.

At Albertsons we gather
essential supplies: popcorn, sodas,
pretzels, chips, and peanut M&M's.

At the Redbox we gather essential movies:
Johnny Depp, Jude Law,
Michael Cera, and Jon Heder
(because we all have a weak spot
for the skinny, homely, Leftover,
Napoleon Dynamites of the world).

## *Temporary Tattoos*

Just after ten,
we unroll our sleeping bags,
slip into our pj's.

"What happened to you?" I ask Katie
as she emerges from the bathroom
in a baby-doll nightie.

"Sharpie fight," she replies,
showing off the red, black, and green marks
on her arms and chest.
"With Angelo."

"You lost?" I ask.

"No! He has an entire ninja battle
drawn on his stomach."

"And you?"

Katie turns, lifts up her nightie,
and peels back her panties.

Olive gasps and covers her eyes.
Carolina explodes into a fit of giggles.
While Emily and I simply gawk.

On her ass, above her tattoo,
is the letter *I*
(her tattoo is the kanji for "love")
and under it,
lettered in awkward capitals,
*ANGEL.*

## Slumber Party Interruptus

Danny walks into the living room,
in his hot body and pajama bottoms,
and joins Carolina in laughing
at Em and me peering at Katie's ass.

Olive tugs Katie's nightgown
back into place.

"Who's Angel?" Danny asks.

"My übercute boyfriend, Angelo," Katie explains,
not at all fazed that Danny saw her bottom.
Sure, it was only for a millisecond. But still.
"I've got pictures," she says, eager to share.

Danny joins her on the couch,
admiring the photos on her cell phone.
"Hispanic?" he asks.

"Puerto Rican," Katie agrees.

"Sorry," he says.
"But evidence suggests,
   that boy is no angel."

## *Tearjerker*

I can tell Emily doesn't
want to talk about boys
because she is crawling
backward into her shell.

I sit next to her
and ask her opinion
about which movie to watch.
She chooses *Chocolat*,
probably not
because of Johnny Depp.
But, I think, because
she knows how it ends,
and that it
will be okay to cry
when the grandmother dies.

# The Truth about Emily

When Katie and I were in seventh grade
we'd relish the moments when we stepped aside
to let Emily Townsend-Smith pass us in the hall
because
    she had curves where we were flat
    she had highlights where our hair was frizzy
    she had confidence where we were clumsy.

When I told Mom
I wanted curves, highlights, and confidence,
she said I should feel sorry for Emily Townsend-Smith
because
    girls whose bodies grew up
    before their minds could catch up
    have a hard time in life.

When Katie and I were in eighth grade
and mobs of sevies
didn't part like the Red Sea when we walked by,
we watched
    Emily Townsend-Smith, the freshman,
    flirt with the varsity quarterback, a senior,
    in the food court at the mall.

When Katie and I were freshmen,
and Emily Townsend-Smith sat beside us
in ninth-grade math, science, and global studies,
she wore
    baggy sweatshirts and corduroys,
    sneakers and kneesocks,
    her hair in a ponytail, sans highlights.

And she was as pretty as we remembered,
just fragile sad crushed,
hiding
    a year behind her peers.
    Never able to escape
    the loss of her virginity and her baby the year before.

## The Truth about Danny

After the sleepover,
Danny was more than some
gadget | appliance | addition
to my house.

I guess I have
Katie to thank for that.
Because she welcomed him
into her world with one
sweet, silly gesture.

I overheard them talking
about how we reminded Danny
of his high school friends—
all of them straight girls.

"Your friends were *Leftovers*?"
Katie asked.

"Leftovers?" Danny echoed.

"Individuals who don't fit
  into any one category."

        "We were like that," he said.
        "We called ourselves floaters—
          drifting from sports
          to theater to cheerleading
          to what have you."

"You were a *cheerleader*?"

        "Nope," Danny said.
        "But I took one to prom."

## My Best Friend Is the Best

After school Katie and I
take over my kitchen table,
spreading out
notebooks, sketchbooks,
manga, and markers.

We play her iPod
over Dad's speakers
and let J-pop mingle
with Bowling for Soup
and the Violent Femmes.

We write and draw
then trade notebooks
and let words mingle
with line, shape,
and color.

## Then Again

I feel bad
about not calling Katie
when Linus and I broke up.

Sure, she was right,
I *was* a crap girlfriend.
And I felt awful enough
without her being there
to rub it in.

But the weird thing was
that I had gotten used to
not telling Katie everything.

I didn't tell her about
making out with J.D.
in the summerhouse
and my very own
not-so-misplaced back rub.

I didn't call her when
we pulled into the driveway

after seven months
of summer vacation.

I guess I was used
to keeping my secrets
to myself.

## Out of Habit

I tie on my sneakers,
step into the brisk weather,
and attempt to regain my sanity
or lose it completely.

Most of the time,
Danny comes running after me
because he thinks that the Greenbelt,
Julia Davis Park, and the Boise State campus
are crawling with crazy people.

Thank God
he gets that I'm not always
in the mood to talk.

Unless it's to complain about
how my teachers are annoying,
my homework assignments impossible,
and my grades dismal.

## Driven

Dad took me
to the DMV,
made a big show
of picking up
a driver's manual.

He made me
flash cards
about stopping,
and yielding,
and turning left.

Danny bought me
a remote control car
and has me parallel parking
between
cereal boxes.

Teaching me
to drive
has become

a friendly competition
between them.

And I'm
soaking up
the attention.

## One Sunday Morning

"What?" Danny asks me. "No run?"

I look down at my pajamas.
I'd been thinking about pancakes
smothered in maple syrup,
coffee with a swirl of cream—
not running.

I look out the kitchen window.
And think about the crisp morning,
wrapped in a blanket of new snow;
our footprints would be the only ones—
not a soul in sight.

"I'll run," I tell Danny. "One minute."

I pull on sweats and sneakers.
And we step out into the cold,
already immersed in conversation,
about how breakfast will taste better
once we've earned it.

"And Dad?" I ask. "Sleeping in?"

"We shouldn't wake him," Danny says.
"I like these runs being just the two of us—
you and me getting to know one another."

"So you don't mind me complaining?"

"Not one bit."

# Report Card

Dad sits me down
on the couch
for a heart-to-heart
about my grades.

He wasn't surprised
that I had pretty much failed
my classes here in Boise
because I had
spent 99 percent of the semester
in New Hampshire.

But he doesn't want to see Ds

ever

again.

# So I Make a Study Date with Katie

But she doesn't show up.
Doesn't answer her phone.
So I stomp over to her house.

"Katie's at Linus's practicing," her mom says.

My best friend forgot about me?
And she's hanging out with my ex-boyfriend!

I tromp to his place and lean on the bell.
Linus's oldest brother answers, baby on his hip.

"Katie here?" I ask him.

"Huh?"

"Katie Raskolnikov? The girl in the band?"

"Who are you, anyway?"

"It's me, Roland. Marcie."

"Dammmn," he drawls in slow disbelief
as he tilts his head and studies me.

"Can I come in?"

"No wonder Linus is totally bummed . . .
little Marcie's a hottie."

I half ignore him and clomp up the stairs.
The familiar notes of "Blister in the Sun"
greet me when I step into the bonus room.
Ian, Linus, and Katie don't look up
from their instruments and Linus starts to sing,

"When I'm out walking I strut my stuff . . .
let me go on—" Linus stops midsentence.

"Big hands I—" Katie cuts the riff.

"Hi, Marcie," Linus says.

"Oh my God!" Katie says.
"I'm so sorry. I forgot about you."

## Outside on the Thomases' Front Steps Katie Reveals

"It is so hard, for me
to be in the middle of all of this.
Linus, Ian, and Angelo
are all calling you a selfish bitch.

So I, well, I—
I haven't invited you
over when they're over—
and I can't invite you
to hang out at the Thomases'."

    "Let me get this straight?
    You've been hanging out
    with the Leftovers,
    without me?"

"We have to practice."

    "For what?"

"The talent show."

I remember them doing that last year.

"And it's weird because
Linus and Emily are
kinda going out."

      "And you didn't tell me?"

"No, I didn't!" she shouts.

      "He's going out with Emily,
       calling me a selfish bitch,
       and you didn't tell me?"

"Like you told me about breaking up with Linus?
Like you told me about kissing Prince Harry?
Like you tell me anything!"

      "I wanted to—"

"But you didn't.
Because you're a
selfish bitch!"

## I Gasp

"Oh God, oh God, oh—"

I shake her words off of me
and
run
all
the
way
home.

| | |
|---|---|
| Katie follows me. | I let myself in. |
| She pounds on the door. | I lean against it. |
| "I'm sorry," she explains.<br>"I didn't mean it." | My shoulders shake. |
| "It just came out." | My eyes sting. |
| "Please, Marcie?<br>I'm sorry." | Sobs choke in my throat. |

She sounds like she
wants to cry.

I bury my cries
in the crook of my arm.

She dials her phone.

The kitchen phone rings.

I run to my room.

I pull my pillow
over my head.

# The House Is Quiet

When I wake up my room is dark.
I can see the red numbers on my clock,
the purplish glow of the neighbor's porch light.

I stumble to the kitchen with the awkward steps
of a sleepwalker in search of Cheerios.
I eat them in front of the silent, gray TV, imagining
myself spilling my guts to millions of viewers
on a daytime confessional.

Linus, J.D., and Katie would all be there
pointing out every terrible thing I have done.

I couldn't argue. They'd be right.

The host would stop for a commercial break.
"Don't worry," he'd say to the camera,
"we'll be back with more selfish bitch,
right after this."

## That's How Danny Found Me

wrapped in a blanket
with a bowl of congealed cereal
on my knees.

"Hey, Marcie," he said when he came home from work.
"You don't look so good."

I shook my head,
wiped my nose on my sleeve.

He sat on the couch,
put his arm over my shoulders,
and pulled me to him.

Fat tears welled in my eyes
and fell on his shirt.

# I Tell Danny

"My friends think I'm a selfish bitch."

"Well," Danny says,
"*selfish* isn't a bad word.
It means 'looking out for
your own interests.'
And, for how crazy life
gets sometimes,
that's a good policy."

"Come on, Danny,
you're just trying to make me feel better."

"*Bitch*, though. That's a tough one."

"I cheated on my boyfriend.
So I guess it fits."

"Ah," he says, like it all makes sense now.
"The male ego bruises easier than a overripe apricot."

"I didn't mean to do it.
I was lonely.
And I didn't know
he loved me."

"It sounds like both of you got hurt—
it'll take some time to get over this."

"Daddy says time and love
cure everything."

"Don't tell Ethan I said
this, but I think what
he means is time and *understanding*
cure everything.

It sounds like *love* started this mess."

## Loner

Wednesday,
I go through the cafeteria line
and buy myself milk
and a chocolate chip cookie
to go with the turkey sandwich
Dad made me.

Then I find a chair
at a mostly empty table
in the corner

because I can't stand
the thought of sitting
with the Leftovers
while they call me names
in their minds.

## Danny Suggested That I Try to Be Understanding

So, before the bell rings,
signaling the end of lunch,
I visit the Leftovers.

"Em, Linus, I know you don't need my blessing,
but I wanted to let you know . . ."

Emily listens intently

while Linus pretends not to hear.

". . . I'm okay with you two going out.
I understand that I haven't been around,
and even though we just broke up,
we've really been apart for seven months."

"You're not mad?" Em asks.

"No," I tell her, Linus, and everyone else.
"We broke up. I'm over him . . . you."

He glances at me when I say "you,"
then away quickly,
as if the word stung his cheek.

"You sure?" Emily confirms.

"Yeah, I'm sure. You deserve Linus,
more than I ever did."

## Eight Seconds Later

Walking away,
I knew
I had said the right thing,
even if
Linus looked like
I dug his heart
out with a spoon.

# Eight Hours Later

I feel like shit.
Being nice sucks.

I shouldn't have done it.
I shouldn't have gift-wrapped Linus for Emily.

I should have said,

"WAIT!

I'm not finished.
I'm not done.

I've got hormones pulsing in my veins,
a broken heart that hasn't healed,
lonely arms that need someone to hold,
and a pair of lips that can't forget That Kiss.

I need him."

## When I Was in New Hampshire

I wanted to come home.

But now that I'm home,
I miss the pine trees, the ocean, the winding roads. . . .

Okay. I'm lying.
I miss J.D.
And Mom.

Not that Dad isn't cool about almost everything.
He's a really good listener.
Not that Danny is an eyesore to eat breakfast with.
He can't wait to teach me how to drive.
It's just really weird getting to know two gay people,
when I've never had any gay friends.

I guess falling in love feels the same
for gay couples.

But I don't even know
what falling in love feels like for me.

Much less anyone else.

## My Best Friend Is Falling in Love

Katie and Angelo
look so darn cute holding hands,
walking to class,
kissing on the steps,
and finishing each other's sentences
like a married couple.

I know for a fact
Katie and Angelo
have managed to get Sharpie marks
nearly everywhere.

I just wish
Katie and I were talking
again.

So I could live vicariously
and feel what it feels like
to fall

in love.

## Mom Calls Me

"I got so bored in Durham,
I drove down to Boston," she said,
like I didn't already know
how boring it is in East Nowhere, New Hampshire.

"That's great!"

"I parked my car at Greta's and got a T-Pass for the week.
I've been to Newbury Street,
Faneuil Hall, and Quincy Market.
The Mary Baker Eddy Library has this Mapparium—
a three-story glass globe. . . ."

I hadn't heard her sound so happy
since the day we went out for Chinese
in our party dresses.

I should have felt happy for her.
But part of me wished
I had been exploring Boston with her,
instead of being here
when she was there.

## Talented

I didn't pay much attention
to the winter talent show
posters in the halls.

I guess
Katie, Linus, and Ian
made the cut
because their band name,
The Leftover Lovers,
is in the program
that the student usher hands me
when I file into the auditorium
for a Friday afternoon assembly.

## Four-Letter Words

Linus has

L O V E

written on the knuckles of his right hand

and

H A T E

written on his left.

Katie has

O V E R

written on the knuckles of her left hand

and

L E F T

written on her right.

## Judging from the Roar of the Crowd

The Leftover Lovers
just won the winter talent show,
with a Bowling for Soup cover,

giving them the honor
of headlining
the Saturday night performance.

(Which means they can play
an entire set.)

I clap politely
as Linus, Katie, and Ian
hug, jump, and whoop onstage

but my heart isn't in it.

## The Saturday Show

is a sold-out event.
The auditorium is packed
with students, family, and friends.

Carolina, Emily, Olive, and I
squeeze into front-row seats
Garrett and Angelo
saved for us.

I sit on the end next to Garrett,
because part of me wants to be one of the Leftovers
and part of me knows I'm almost unwelcome.

Although we clap and cheer
for the other acts,
we're really here to hear
a few Bowling for Soup
and Violent Femmes covers
by The Leftover Lovers.

The curtains open to Ian's drumroll,
revealing Katie and Linus
center stage.

One mike.

Linus is in dark jeans, black Converse,
a hand-me-down Superman T-shirt,
and the faintest smudge of eyeliner.

Katie's wearing a blue button-down, Doc Martens,
a Catholic schoolgirl skirt over thigh-high stockings,
and a black garter belt.

Angelo puts two fingers between his lips
and whistles.

Katie flips her pink-streaked hair
and blows him a kiss.

The crowd erupts in cheers.

## Linus Looks So Cute

hiding his nervousness
behind his bangs
by pretending to watch
his fingers work the chords.

(But I know he can play "Blister" with his eyes closed.)

Then he looks up,
shakes his bangs out of the way,
and sings into the mike.

I'm not kidding you.
Girls screamed.

## Midset

After "Blister in the Sun,"
they play two Son of Dork songs,
"Ticket Outta Loserville"
and a somber rendition of "Party's Over."

Katie backs away from the mike.
Linus sings alone:

> *I just watched my girlfriend get laid on the sofa*
> *Does that seem weird to you?*

Emily, I think.
He chose this song because of Emily.

> *It's complicated*
> *Stranded at first base I never saw her naked*

Me, I think.
He chose this song because of me?

*Ouch.*

# "The Next Song Isn't a Cover"

Linus announces into the mike,
over the roar of the crowd.
"It's a little something I wrote
to play tonight.
I call it
'The Dr. Seuss Breakup Song'!"

He counts out loud, unleashing
pulsing amps and pounding drums.

> *Leave me alone. Get out of my head.*
> *Stop patching things up, get out of my bed.*
> *Walk the other way, get out of my face.*
> *Don't say good-bye, turn your back instead.*
>
> *I need to breathe. I need some space.*
> *No, I don't want to talk. Don't want an embrace.*
> *I don't care if you cry, don't care if you pout.*
> *We don't belong. We're a disgrace.*
>
> *Leave me alone, I shout.*
> *I want you gone. I want you out.*

*Don't email, don't text, don't telephone.*
*It's over, my love, beyond a doubt.*

*I gave you my heart, now turned to stone.*
*I gave you my flesh, I gave you my bones.*
*It wasn't enough. It didn't work out.*
*Get out of my head. Leave me alone.*

## After the Applause

Linus doesn't stop playing,
he just morphs the chords
into a minor key,
slows the rhythm
to that of a relaxed heartbeat.

> Alone in my room, hand in hand, side by side
> I said, "I love you," and you replied,
> "But there is something you must be told."
> With those words you cannot hide.

> I thought I would cherish the day
> that I gave my heart away,
> but you pushed it back, closed my chest
> with nothing but willpower gone astray.

> You say you were lonely, unwanted, cold.
> That he was just a body to hold.
> "It was different there, on Little Bay,"
> on and on you list your reasons bold.

I thought I would cherish the day
that I gave my heart away,
but you pushed it back, closed my chest
with nothing but willpower gone astray.

The truth is too much to digest,
leaves me heavy, motionless, depressed.
"But I love you," I cry as you get dressed.
"I love you," I shout, a man obsessed.

## Standing Ovation

"Fuck you!" I shout at Linus.
"If you wanted to talk to me,
  all you had to do was call!"

But he doesn't hear me among
the clapping whooping stomping.

He's holding Katie's hand.
They're taking a bow.

I storm out.

Before anyone
can see that

I'm crying.

# The Auditorium Door

clanks shut behind me,
muffling whistles shouts cheers.
I lean against it,
sink to the floor.

Thoughts thud in my head
to the rhythm of the drums
as Ian starts in on an encore

Now
    The whole school knows I broke his heart.
    That I'm a slut. A crap girlfriend.
    They know that my best friend hates me.
    Or she wouldn't be in the band,
    playing along to my ex-boyfriend's tune.

    I'm no longer a Leftover.
    How could I be?
    No one even likes me.

I feel as if
I am on one side

of a two-inch-thick barricade
and the rest of the world
is on the other.

# The First Letter I Don't Send

Dear Linus,

I'm glad that you
got me off your chest.
It must have been therapeutic.

Why else would you bring up
everything
I've ever done,
every emotion
you've ever felt
in front of the whole school?

Maybe now you can move on,
and be the kind of guy Emily deserves.

God knows she doesn't need
to date a rebounding loser
like you.

Go to hell,
Marcie

# P.S.

I hate you and
everything I've ever done
to make you hate me.

# The Second Letter I Don't Send

Dear Katie,

How could you?

How could you
play all those notes
when you knew
the lyrics
would hit my heart
like buckshot
    carefully packed
    into a shotgun shell
    and fired point-blank?

You knew, you had to know.

Your former best friend,
Marcie

## Period

I hurt all over.

My head throbs from crying,
my stomach knots with cramps,

my body bleeds as if my insides are wounded,
and my ego aches for redemption.

Forget the Midol,
could someone please
pass the Prozac?

## Katie Hasn't

called
IM'd
emailed
stopped by
or said hi.

## I Think

the
whole
world
hates
me.

# The Downside of Living with Dad and Danny

There is no one
    to go to the store
    and buy you tampons.
No one who knows
    you need the kind with applicators
    because you can't figure out the other ones.
No one who knows
    you like the regular size, unscented
    because you don't want to smell like a baby's
        bottom.
So I go to the grocery store
    to buy a magazine, a Coke, a candy bar,
    a bag of chips, English muffins, peanut butter,
    and tampons.
I carefully choose a female cashier,
    then pile my items on the conveyor belt
    so you can't see the tampons.
She swipes the items,
    the register beep-beeping,
    and slides them back to the bagging area—
    the tampons exposed.

Ducking my blushing face,
  I pay with a twenty, stuff my change in my pocket.
  I reach for my two plastic bags without looking up.

My fingers tangle with the bag boy's,
  the bags' handles twisting us together.

      "Need help out, Marcie?"

I look up to see Linus. "No."

        He asks if I am sure, handing me one bag
        and keeping the other one hostage.

"Really. I walked," I snap.

        He walks next to me anyway,
        looking shy in his Day-Glo orange vest.

"So you got a job?" I try to be nicer.

        "Yeah. My dad lost his in the layoffs.
        So I've gotta cover my music lessons."

We reach the edge of the parking lot

        and Linus says,
          "I'm sorry . . . about the songs."

"They kicked me in the gut," I tell him.
"But I guess that was the point."

          "It was a stupid stunt—
            to get my revenge in front of everyone—
            I shouldn't have done it."

"Apology accepted," I say,
 consciously trying not to be selfish.
 Or a bitch.

## Things I Threw Away

Seeing Linus at the grocery store
just reminded me
how much I like him.

Really.

I had him.
I had everything.
I had his heart
    (but didn't know it).
He loved me.

Past tense.

## *He Reminds Me*

I want to be somebody
    (not famous, or rich,
    or even beautiful)
just somebody to someone.

I want another person to notice me,
    to say that I matter,
    to say that they care
about me.

    Like J.D. did.

Is that so wrong? Selfish?

## My Girl

If my mom says
women
are not property

how come I want
to belong
to someone?

## All Week

I wait
for Katie to apologize

(even just a little)

for playing in the band,
when all the songs were about me,

(or maybe)

for not telling me that
all the songs on the set list were breakup songs
and that I should have come wearing emotional armor.

(So what)

if she thinks I'm a selfish bitch.
There's a limit. Even selfish bitches don't deserve that.

(I mean)

Linus apologized for the songs.
And we aren't even best friends.

## What I'd Say to Katie

(IF WE WERE TALKING)

We're best friends.                    Right.
You tell me everything.                Right.

I'd do anything for you.
I'd walk on coals for you.
I'd lie to your mom for you.

You'd skip study hall                  Right.
to buy me Midol.                       Right.

I'd hold your hand.
I'd take a stand.
I'd walk with you to Neverland.

You'd wipe my tears.                    Right.
We'll be friends for years.            Right?

## Temper Tantrum

When I was little
and I got home from school
before my mom got home from work,
I'd throw myself on the sofa,
kick scream wail        "I want my mommy!"
until she came home.

Somehow,
it worked every time.

But today when I called her,
hoping for an ear that would listen
to my never-ending list of problems,
she didn't pick up.

I wanted to
shout cry sob        "I miss my mommy!"

but I left her a message
instead.

## No One Can Hurt My Heart
## Inside My Little Ball

I curl up into a ball
to protect my breaking heart.

My ball isn't small enough.

I curl up into a little ball.

All alone
fat ugly unloved little ball.

All alone
stupid careless selfish little ball.

All alone
crying confused hopeless little bawl.

## I Am to Blame

I was the one
who felt all alone.
The one who would do anything
to make the emptiness go away.

I was the one
who stumbled into J.D.'s arms.
The one who kissed and touched
just to get a fix.

I was the one
who broke Linus's heart
by reaching out
to save my own from shriveling up.

I was the one
who didn't email, IM, or telephone.
The one who told the truth
too late.

I was the one
who put Katie in the middle.

The one who tried to
make her choose.

I won't say I'm the one who broke up the Leftovers—
even though it feels like I did.
Because Leftovers, of all people,
need to listen to each other,
care about one another,
and understand.

Even if it's difficult.

## Because I Want My Best Friend Back

I plunk my butt next to Katie's on the bus.
"I get that you're mad at me," I say.
"But I don't know why."

"Duh."

"I broke up with Linus, not you."

"And he blames me," she says.

"Why?"

"Because I told you that falling in love
feels like that jolt right before you fall asleep."

"Yeah," I agree.

"But Linus says it's like springtime on the moon.
All sunshine and cherry blossoms but no gravity."

"What's he smoking?" I ask.
"That doesn't make sense."

"That's what I said," Katie goes on.
"But Linus says if I had explained
what falling in love *really* felt like,
you would have known that you loved him,
not the Prince of New Hampshire."

"I didn't fall in love with either of them."

"When you do fall in love?" she asks.
"Will you tell me?"

"Yeah." I bump her shoulder with mine.
"What are best friends for?"

## You're Invited

Linus hands out invitations to the Leftovers.
They are decorated with fire engines and Dalmatians.

Who: Emily's Baby Boy

What: First Birthday

When: Saturday, February 3, 1:00 p.m.

Where: Katie's House

*Your presence is our present!*

## Saturday, 1:00 P.M.

On Saturday, I walk to Katie's
in time to see Linus pull in the drive.
(I didn't know he got his license.)
He gets out and steps around.

In her car seat, his niece cries raindrops.

"Shush, Bug. Really now,"
  he says as he unbuckles her.
"Aunt Marcie's here,
  don't you want to wave hi-hi?"

She giggles.
And so do I,
because Linus just implied
that we were married.

"Bug is the substitute for Emily's baby,"
Linus explains, handing me her diaper bag.

## Childish Games

We play games meant for kids
younger than us by years—
duck-duck-goose,
Chutes and Ladders,
Candy Land,
and Twister.

Bug crawls around, wide-eyed.
Wondering, probably, why all the laughter?

She isn't sure what to think
of the Mylar balloons,
the crepe paper streamers,
of her uncle and the Leftovers.

She decides that the party,
most certainly, is for her

because she doesn't
see any other baby,
just her friend Emily,
sitting out.

## Roller Coaster

"Em?" I ask, pulling my chair close to hers.
"Is all of this really okay with you?"
    (I think it's really weird
    to celebrate an adopted baby's birthday,
    when he isn't here.)

Em looks at me.
Tears have tracked shiny lines down her pretty face.
    (I'm ready to call the whole thing off,
    whisk her away, feed her orange juice,
    chicken soup, and One A Day vitamins.)

        "Yeah." She nods.
        "I'm saying good-bye to my baby."

"You sure?" I ask again.

        "Uh-huh, it's part of my grieving process.
         Sharon, my therapist,
         says it's okay to feel emotions."

"Like all of them? All at once?" I ask.
(Olive, Ian, Carolina, and Katie collapse
into a giddy giggling mess on the Twister mat.)

"Happy and sad."
Emily nods, then smiles.

"All mixed up," I say,
and wrap her in a hug.

## Flame

Katie's mom dims the lights,
brings in a cupcake and candle.

In the flickering candlelight,
we sing "Happy Birthday" to Emily's baby.

Sitting on Linus's lap, Bug spies the flame
and bursts into tears because the food is on fire.

"It's okay, my little friend,"
Katie's mom explains.

Emily blows out the candle
and says, "One year down."

Emily's giggles turn to tears
as Bug's tears turn to giggles.

# To Love, To Family, To Friends

Katie's mom makes a toast,
to family and to friends.

"I want to thank Emily,
on behalf of adoptee families everywhere,
for her selfless gift.
The gift of life
that makes families like ours complete.

We love our daughter, Katie,
like the parents of Em's baby love him.
So much—so much I can't explain."

"I love Katie, too,"
Angelo announces,
wrapping his arms around her.

I look at Linus holding Bug—
both sticky with frosting.

And think he's the one.
Not just for silly parties,

Candy Land and Twister,
but for all the times in between.

There, watching Linus
feed Bug bits of cupcake,
I decide
to patch up my mistakes, his heart.

To make mortar out of tears.

# I've Changed My Mind, All I Want Is Everything

I want respect.        I will respect.
I want love.           I will love
I want passion.                with passion.

# A Conversation for Adults

When I tell Mom that
my friend Emily
has a therapist named Sharon,

      she says, "That's good."

"Maybe what is good for Emily
would be good for you, too," I suggest.

      "Yes, I should talk to a counselor.
      But I have to take my meds, too."

"Meds?"

      "I suffer from depression, Marcie."

"I know, I mean, I noticed."

      "So I need to take antidepressants."

"Are you?"

"I've started again." She sighs.

"But you weren't?"

    "No. Not after your dad . . .
    um, made his announcement.
    I just took the Ambien. Not the others."

"Why not?"

    "Because I wanted to feel something—
    my husband left me for a
    twenty-seven-year-old man
    and all I felt was numb."

"Huh?"

    "My meds build this barrier
    between me and my emotions—
    leaving me without a backstage pass."

"You wanted to feel bad?"

"I was depressed.
I couldn't see straight, think straight."

"You could have told me.
I could have called the doctor.
I could have helped—"

She says, "I'm sorry, Marcie,"
her voice all shaky.
"I didn't know how to ask for help.
I didn't realize that you'd understand."
She sniffles.

My lower lip starts to tremble
and I grip the receiver,
as if it were her hand.

## Revelations

"Don't cry, Mommy," I say,
  because hearing her sob is breaking my heart.

      "I wasn't a good mom, was I?"

"Everybody makes mistakes."

      "But I'm the parent."

"Not even parents are perfect."

      "Ethan is. I hated that,
        always trying to be his storybook bride.
        I couldn't do it."

"Daddy doesn't seem
  like he expected much."

      "No, I just felt like he was too good for me—
        because I had to see a psychotherapist
        and take medicine just to get by."

## Mom Plans to Come for a Visit

She says she won't stay too long—
that she's looking for a job in Boston
and has to move in with Aunt Greta
before the first of March,
but she'll come see me.

I don't care
what she's planning
as long as she's here.

Even if
it is
just for a little while.

# My Mother Always Told Me

that women could be anything they wanted to be
    mayor | governor | senator | president

But I guess it never occurred to her that I'd act like
    a player | a frat boy | my father | Bill Clinton

Then again, I don't think it was part of her plan to be
    a thief | a kidnapper | addicted | depressed

She certainly thought I was above depending on boys for
    doughnuts | coffee | companionship | acceptance

Instead I had turned to J.D. to make me feel
    worthwhile | beautiful | sexy | happy

And hurt someone who loved me because I was
    careless | insensitive | mean | self-centered

Now that I am man-free, Mom would probably say
that I have achieved some sort of feminist
    Zen | pride | accomplishment | freedom

But no matter how hard I try, I still yearn for
hugs | kisses | smiles | a hand to hold.

## Wishful Thinking

Today I was looking at Linus
    in that way girls look at guys,
    watching his actions,
    his body,
    his hands,
    listening to the timbre of his voice
    (and not hearing the words),
    watching his eye movement,
just in case our eyes should meet
for a brief moment
in time.

## What My Ex-Boyfriend Doesn't Know

I have the
biggest crush

on him.

## On One Side

Seeing Linus at the bus stop,
slouched on Katie's couch while we study,
in the cafeteria, pushing ketchup around his plate,
starts an emotional tug-of-war.

I'm on one side rooting for Emily
    (because she deserves the nicest guy on planet Earth).

As Emily's cheerleader I want her to win.
    (She deserves a decent boyfriend.)
But she keeps dropping passes
    (turning her head away from a direct on-the-lips kiss)
fumbling the ball
    (letting go of his hand to tuck her hair behind her ear)
and faking left instead of running right
    (making excuses every time he invites her somewhere).

The only thing she and Linus do together
    is babysit his niece.
    And it's okay. I've done that, too.
But you can only get so much kissing done
    between bottles, baths, and binkies.

## On the Other Side

I'm on the other side
  (wanting Linus back).

When I root for my team, I want to win.
  (Because I deserve a rematch).
I receive every serve
  (smiling when he says hello to me)
return every volley
  (talking about the weather when he offers one word)
and covet every match
  (hoping to shake the "ex-girlfriend"
  label and trade it in for "friend").

The only things Linus and I do together
  are wait for the bus,
  eat lunch (well, I eat, anyway), and
  study at Katie's with the Leftovers.
But you can only get so much conversation in
  between buses, bells, and books.

## Every Morning at the Bus Stop

I say hello to Linus,
like back in eighth grade,
when we hung out in his room
for hours.

"Brrr," he says,
his breath forming steam
in the frostbitten air.

hoping that someday,
we can be friends again,
and talk about everything
just because.

"Cold," I agree.
"But at least,
 it's gonna be sunny."

## Just Silence

Katie and I
spread our notebooks and pencils across the coffee table
to write, draw, and eat chocolate chip cookies.

Although we're quiet,
I know we're going to be okay.
No more fighting. No more blame. No more tears.

I know because we're spending time together, alone.
Before the Leftovers come over to study for a history test.

## Studying at Katie's House

Linus sits next to me on the couch,
oddly close, but distant.

Sometimes his knee touches mine,
the soft fringes of torn denim tickling my bare skin.

Maybe it is too close, too soon,
but I enjoy every minute.

# *I Can't Find My Blue Notebook*

I must have left it at Katie's.

I know it's safe.

Katie would guard my secrets
with an army of anime ninja girls
with shadow-clone *jutsu* powers
who'd leap into action

if anyone tried to read
my poems.

## Today at the Bus Stop

"Your cheeks are pink," Linus says.

My heart beats once.

He steps closer.

I hold my breath.

He takes his hands from his pockets.

And touches my face.

He caresses my cheeks
as if to warm them.

I search his eyes
as if, in them, I could read his thoughts.

Longing? Tenderness? Love?
Okay, so I'm not so good at reading minds.

Except my own.
Longing? Check.

Desire? Check.
Lust? Check.
Heartbeat? Check.

I reach up,
wrap my cold fingers around his warm neck,
and pull his face down toward mine.

At that moment, I decide
I must be dreaming
because he's not resisting or pulling away.

I kiss his lips, his mouth.
Hungry for him, for heat,
for the stolen moment in dreamland
before he realizes I am not Emily.

He pulls me close.

Air whooshes from my parka.

Our mouths press on.

Tasting like toothpaste and Scope.

"God, Marcie," he whispers
 prayers into my lips.

       I pray that my alarm clock
       doesn't run out of snooze.

"Shit," Linus says. "The bus."

       Linus doesn't swear in my dreams.

## Sitting Down

In Boise,
we don't ride school buses
in high school.
So Linus and I
slide our cards
through the city bus
fare box.

We step past commuters,
the usual kids from earlier stops.
There's one seat
and Linus motions
for me to take it.

I do. Even though
I'd rather
sit on his knee
like I used to—
his arms around me
like a seat belt.

I tug on his sleeve, whisper,
"What just happened?"

He bends close.

"That," he says in my ear,

"was amazing."

## A Moment of Truth

"Does that mean, that you and I—"

"Not so fast," Linus warns,
caution written in his voice.
"There's one more thing
you need to know."

And from his backpack,
he removes a blue notebook.

"It's yours.

I read it."

## My Notebook

Immediately, I know the notebook's contents:
    poems about love, lust, and loneliness,
    docks, fires, and gravel lanes,
    big panties and condoms,
    blue dresses and rocking canoes,
    talent shows and selfish bitches,
    quiet crushes and candlelit cupcakes.

"I picked it up by accident—
    at Katie's when we were studying.

I didn't plan on reading it,
    but I couldn't help myself."

# The Cry of a Thousand Years

Somewhere inside me
the dammed-up storm

    of missing Linus
        and not knowing if he liked me
        enough to touch me

    of kissing J.D.
        and leaving him in New Hampshire
        like an unwanted puppy

    of losing Katie
        and wondering if we'd ever be friends again

    of wanting back
        what I had to begin with: Linus

begins to overflow,
    and tears streak down my cheeks.
    I stand up, fling myself into his arms.

He cups one hand over my head,
     and pulls me to his shoulder,
     shushing me with quiet lullabies
     as we sway to the motion of the bus.

## Even Though It's Not Our Stop

Linus takes my hand,
leads me down the aisle,
down the steps.

The bus rolls away,
leaving us in the privacy
of a dark winter morning.

"People were staring,"
he explains, handing me
my notebook.

I take it from him,
fold it
in my arms
over my beating heart—
as if
to shield myself
with the one thing
that made me
most
vulnerable.

## Question

"You didn't happen to skip
the one about
me holding you close
under the covers
with only
a condom
between us?"

Linus smiles
and says
he wouldn't have
missed it for the world.

And that he read that one
twice.

## Rebellion

"Let's go," he says.

"The next bus is coming."
I nod in the direction
of a bus stopped at a light.
"We can take that."

"Not to school," he explains.

A thrill shoots though me
as we join hands
                    and
                        take
                            off
                                running
                                    toward
                                        downtown.

## Three Choices

Crying and running gave me the hiccups
so I am a snotty hiccupping mess
when Linus sits me on a couch in a coffee shop.

He hands me a napkin
and says, "I'll be right back."

But eight a.m. is coffee rush hour
and the line snakes from the counter to the door.

Alone in the crowd,
I smooth my fingers over my notebook's cover,
over the lopsided loops of wire that hold it together,
over the ballpoint-pen ripples on the inside pages.

Slowly, it sinks in.
That Linus read my notebook.

Like an annoying little brother.
Or a parent convinced their child
is having sex or smoking pot.

My primitive monkey brain
wants to hit him upside the head,
shout at the top of my lungs,
"You had no right!"

My logical analytical brain
reasons that reading a notebook
isn't nearly as bad as
kissing J.D. without my shirt on.

My infatuated insistent heart
and my kiss-happy lips
want me to run up behind Linus,
put my arms around his waist,
and squeeze.

So I do.

## *Over Coffee and a Cranberry Scone*

"Does this mean you forgive me?" I ask.

"Yeah," Linus says, leaning closer.

"How come?"

"Because I understand how you felt."

"Yeah, thanks to reading my diary."

"Sorry."

"But aren't you and Emily an item?"

"Em thinks I'm a saint."

"Linus, you *are* a saint."

"That's just it, I'm not," he says.
"Every time I see Em,
  I want to hold her tight.
  But she freezes like

a cardboard cutout of Marilyn Monroe
every time I try."

"That's sad," I say. "Poor Em."

"So I think I understand,
how you felt, a million miles away
without someone to hug you."

## Calculated

"It wasn't easy, forgiving you, I mean," Linus says.

"I guess I never got a chance to tell you
how angry I felt—
how betrayed.

I couldn't quite believe
you chose to be honest
after so many months of deceit.

I tried to calculate
when you might have fallen
away from me
and for J.D.

I tried to calculate
the duration of your lies,
figuring that
the longer you lied,
the worse I'd punish you—
the more my lyrics' whip would sting.

But after I did it,
after you swore at me
and ran from the auditorium,

it occurred to me—
I no longer wanted to hurt you.

I wanted you back."

## Wishing Well

After coffee and breakfast have warmed us up
we head out into the blue-gray morning,
lit by strings of leftover Christmas lights.

Linus puts his arm around me
as we cross the street.
He directs my steps to the frosted-over fountain—
    the water resembling a blue raspberry slushy.

From his pocket, Linus pulls two pennies—
    handing me one. Warm in my palm.

Together we toss
our pennies in,
wishing, maybe,
for the very same thing.

## "My Life Has Been a Hurricane"

I tell Linus as we wait for the light on Front to change.

"Not only did I let it whoosh me
from one side of the country to another,
I let it sweep away my conscience,
turning me into a tropical storm, too.

I darted here and there
without a care in the world—
hurting people, messing up their lives.

All the while, I blamed it on the hurricane,
not myself.

I thought it was your fault
    because you didn't touch me.
I thought it was Dad's fault
    because he wrecked our family.
I thought it was Mom's fault
    because she slept all day.
I thought it was Katie's fault
    because she chose the Leftovers over me.

I couldn't see through the wind and rain and tears.

I couldn't see you loved me
    because I was in New Hampshire
    and you were here.
I couldn't see that Dad was all alone
    in his marriage without anyone to talk to.
I couldn't see that Mom needed meds
    just to set her earth back on its axis.
I couldn't see that I was a horrible best friend
    who demanded unconditional love in return.

I had become the hurricane,
leaving broken hearts,
disappointed parents,
and torn friendships
in my wake."

# Skipping School Never Sounded So Good

In Julia Davis Park,
Linus sings to me from the band-shell stage,
using his fist like a microphone,
my heart thump-thumping the beat:

> *I want to tell you just one thing*
> *You closed me out, I want back in*
> *Give me a chance, give me a spin*
>
> *Don't turn your back, don't walk away*
> *It'll just take a minute to say*
> *I think about you every day*
> *I love you, girl, I'm not gay*
>
> *I didn't love you right, let me try again*
> *You said you wanted real passion*
> *I can give it to you, darlin'*
>
> *Don't turn your back, don't walk away*
> *It'll just take a minute to say*
> *I think about you every day*
> *I love you, girl, I'm not gay*

*Take me back, make me sing*
*I can give it to you, darlin'*
*I can give it to you, darlin'*

I'm his adoring crowd of one,
who giggles uncontrollably
then smothers his little-boy face with kisses.

## Skipping Stones

Linus races me to the riverbank,
and I win.

"You're in good shape," he says, gasping.
"It's just a bad habit I picked up," I tell him.
"I can run three miles."

Linus says, "That's cool,"
picking up a flat, gray stone and whipping it
so it skips       across       the water's       surface.

"Running helped me deal with things . . ."
I tell him, letting my voice trail off
like the       stones       plunk,       plunk,       plunking.

"And I just wrote Dr. Seuss breakup songs,
but       you       know       about       those."

# Tunnel of Love

At the playground,
we play hide-and-seek,
    ducking under too-small gazebos
    slip-sliding on icy metal platforms
    leaping handrails           to get away
    chasing each other up slides and down again
while static electricity stands our hair on end.

I tag his sneaker.
    (As if I couldn't see those telltale All Stars
    sticking out from the end of the red tunnel.)
Rather than scooting out and chasing after me,
he curls one finger in my direction,
calling me closer.

On all fours,
I crawl over him
in slow motion
until my hands are planted at his shoulders,
my knees at his hips.
He smiles up at me, in a toying boyish way
and then pulls me into a head-to-toe embrace.

My body presses against his—
jeans, keys, pockets, parkas
all in between—

yet not there at all.

# In the Library!

"I'm frozen," Linus whispers.

Together we decide the library
would be a warm place to hide.

We sneak up the stairs
and tiptoe deep into the stacks.

*Lub dub | lub dub*

I take his guitar-calloused hands
and cozy them under my sweater
against my beating heart.

*Lub dub | lub dub*

His fingers spread
to span the geography of my body,
ice cubes melting
against moist sweat.

*Lub dub | lub dub*

"I can feel your heartbeat."

"I can hear it," I say.

"Yeah?"

"It's been talking about you."

"What does it say?"

"Love dub | love dub."

## At Zeppole

We only have $4.62 between us,
    so we share a bowl of soup
    and a plate of all-you-can-eat bread.

Linus says he can't miss that history test seventh period,
    and although he claims he isn't a saint,
    he isn't about to mess up his A average.

At the office,
    I explain that my alarm clock never went off
    and I missed the bus, but Linus has his
    license and keys to his brother's car.

And if she didn't mind,
    the secretary could call my dad's boyfriend,
    Danny, and he'd explain everything
    even though he couldn't write me a note,
    being that he isn't my legal guardian or anything.

Somehow that
    gets us back into school.

## In Both of My Classes

my teachers sound like
the one in the *Peanuts* cartoons,
talking gibberish.

Because all I can hear
all afternoon
is my heartbeat
thumping out its new mantra

    *Love dub | love dub*
    *Love dub | love dub*
    *Love dub | love dub*

## After the Last Bell

Linus stops
by my locker.

I notice that he doesn't
kiss, touch, or hug me.

I hope he hasn't
changed his mind.

"I've got to tell Emily," Linus says.
"Before this hits the fan."

And I realize he's doing
what I should have done
the day J.D. kissed me:

tell the truth
before it grew stale.

# Walking Daydreams

I am so happy giddy giddy
I smile at the blue blue sky
and practically skip.

I wish Katie was here
so I could kiss and tell,
gossip about love and fairy tales.

I tell the trees, the squirrels,
the fence posts, the mailbox,
"I'm in love. He loves me."

"I can't quite believe it!
We skipped school to fall in love.
I kissed Linus and he kissed me."

"He's telling Emily
he'd rather just be friends.
He's in love. He loves me."

And she'll admit she liked him
and how he respected her, but
that wasn't love and she understood.

Or maybe she'll say she loved him
and wanted to hold him tight, but
forgot how to do it. Could he show her?

Maybe he'll wrap his arms around her,
feel her curves under her sweater,
and ask, "Can I spend forever here?"

I skid to a stop.
What? Huh?

This is *my* daydream
*my* Cinderella story
*my* first time falling in love.

He can't possibly go running off
with the prettiest girl in school
instead of me!

Can he?

# *Worries*

I try to do my math homework
but end up writing proofs as if they were poetry.

I try to analyze *King Lear*
but end up writing my paper in poems.

I try to work on my biology project
but I end up with poems in my PowerPoint presentation.

Danny asks me, "What's wrong?"
and I tell him that Linus and I skipped school.

"And you're worried about what your dad will think?"

"No. I'm worried
that Linus might not love me
after all—
     that maybe I was just a quick fix.
     A hug and a kiss to tide him over
     until cardboard cutout Emily
     gets wet in the rain
     and decides to bend."

Danny just looks at me
like I don't make any sense
and wonders out loud
if "maybe this is stuff for your notebook?"

## Notes from My Heart

I take my notebook
from my bag.
Smooth my fingers
over pages,
as if the bubbles
made by long-ago tears
were messages
written in Braille.

I start to read
what I had written,
but stop
midsentence

when the
doorbell
rings.

## What Emily Said

Linus has his backpack on,
like he hasn't been home
since before we got off the bus.

"I talked to Emily,
and she admitted
that she isn't ready
for a relationship."

He takes a deep breath.

"And she'd rather
we be friends like before,
except she'd like to
keep her babysitting job."

I can't wait another second.

I grab his backpack straps.
Pull him to me.
Kiss his mouth.
Kiss away any doubt.

## My Dad Comes Home

I stop kissing Linus
and try to regain my balance,
my composure.

Dad puts down his briefcase,
takes off his coat.

Linus ignores him,
looks in my eyes,
and asks me
if I'd be his girlfriend,
again.

"Yes," I say.
"Exclusively."

(Just in time
for Valentine's Day.)

Dad thinks we should celebrate
so he treats us to pizza
at Flying Pie on State Street,

where they play eighties rock
and pinball
instead of watching the Wildcats
play football.

And I like it better.

Even though Linus and Daddy
both beat me at pinball.

## On the Way Home from Pizza

Dad turns down Linus's street
and parks the Mustang in the Thomases' driveway—
his not-so-subtle way of saying I have homework to do.
I flop the front seat forward and wiggle out.

Linus unfolds his long legs and stands up beside me.
He takes my hand, leans down, and kisses my cheek.
"See you at the bus stop."

My heart *love-dub*s in my chest,
not wanting to say good night.

So I shut the car door,
hold up one finger in a promise
that I'll be back in a minute.
Or five.

Linus's hand still in mine,
we walk to his door,
where no one has bothered to turn on a light.

My heart *love-dub*s in my chest.
I think I say, "Kiss me."

But Linus
may have

read my mind.

## Kissing My Boyfriend

feels like riding
a Tilt-A-Whirl.

When I open my eyes,
it takes me a minute
to regain my balance.

"Linus . . ."
I take a deep breath
and say out loud
exactly what my heart
wants my lips to say:

"I love you."

"I love you, too," he says.

## Snuggled in Bed

Long after
Dad's heart-to-heart
about the importance
of school attendance,

I open
my precious
blue spiral notebook
to what
I thought
was a blank page
only to find it
written on!

## Dear Marcie

Some things are inexcusable.
And I just did one of those things.
      I read your notebook.

Go ahead and hate me.
But I had to do it.
You were the first girl I ever loved
      and I had to know where I went wrong.

Yes, I dumped you because you cheated on me.
But after reading your diary,
I realize that I had misunderstood.
I thought you had sex with him.
      And that hurt. A lot.

And, I know you thought I was gay
because I never touched your breasts.
      Believe me, I wanted to.

But part of me wasn't ready to take your clothes off
because I've seen *Maxim*, *Playboy*, and *Hustler*

(that's what happens when you have older brothers)
    and I know that shit ain't real.

I didn't want
my smart, talented, adorable, emotional girlfriend
to turn into a three-dimensional magazine centerfold
    when I peeled off her T-shirt.

I know you're laughing.
But I swear that's what happened to Roland
    and Bug's mom.
They were best friends until they started
    sleeping together
    instead of talking to each other.

And I swore I'd never let that happen to me.

I guess that's what I wanted to tell you.
And if, someday, you get over hating me for reading this
and want to be friends again
    I'd really like that.

Love, Linus

## I Jump Out of Bed and Call Linus

"You wrote me a poem!"

"Not a very good one."
He laughs.

"It's sweet."

"It's embarrassing."

"But now I know for
sure."

"For sure what?"

"That I'm dating the
sweetest guy on earth."

"Dorkiest, maybe."

"Linus!" I complain.

In the background,
Roland agrees.
There's a dull thud,
like someone got hit.

When I'm sure Linus
is back, I say,
"I didn't know you thought
I had sex with J.D."

"I didn't know what to think."

"I guess I didn't tell you
that I *didn't* sleep with him."

"I think you did,
I just couldn't hear you."

"We weren't exactly
talking."

"Next time, I promise
to tell you stuff on the bus.
So the whole city'll know."

"Or in the cafeteria—"

"Gotta make sure
the whole school can hear."

"Or in the auditorium—"

"Into the mike.
Loud and clear,
in case they missed it."

"Or maybe I'll just
write you a poem—
a totally embarrassing
mushy one."

"And I'll write you a
love song—
a sticky sweet one
about kissing you."

"I'd like that."

"Me too."

# On the Last Page of My Notebook

As my mixed-up,
gay-dad-crazy-mom world
returns to its previously scheduled orbit

and the tropical storm that was my life
dwindles to scattered showers,

I close my eyes
and listen to my heartbeat.

*Love dub | love dub*

It sounds like a two-tone metronome,
sending me a message in Morse code.

*Love dub | love dub*

I get it now.
My heart says it's in love.

But it didn't feel like
that jolt before falling asleep
or like springtime on the moon.

It felt like my heart
had something to say,
and all I had to do

was listen.

## *Acknowledgments*

I'd like to thank my agent, Danielle Chiotti, for believing
in my manuscript; my editor, Sarah Shumway, for
making it shine; and Laurel Symonds, Kathryn Hinds,
and Maggie Herold for polishing it. My gratitude goes
out to my crit group at The Cabin, who read the first
draft; to Athena Birckbichler, who worked behind the
scenes; and to Laura Gray, who reassures me that I'm
only as old as I act. Thanks to Sonya Sones for the
inspiration and to the Violent Femmes and Son of Dork
for the tunes. Many thanks to my parents for their support
and encouragement, to my family for the camp and my
New Hampshire roots, and to Jason for everything else.